WOOT !

Janice Lipsky

With illustrations by

Carrie A. Schultz

Dedication

To Richard, who built an aviary.

Contents

Acknowledgements

There are many people I'd like to thank for their support along this journey. Thanks to Mariann Caprino and Gordon Bear, who provided feedback and spurred me on. Thanks to family members who read the work in progress and encouraged me: Myra Hall and Susan Klatsky Cohen. Thanks to middle school expert, Claire Tunick for her excellent critique. Thanks to my fabulous illustrator, Carrie A. Schultz, for her beautiful artwork and collaboration. For information about pigeon rescue, contact Palomacy Pigeon and Dove Adoptions, at PigeonRescue.org.

Preface

Pigeons. For many, the mere word conjures up images of dirty flocks scavenging for food on crowded city streets. Some people even call them "rats of the sky." In fact, pigeons may be the most misunderstood creatures in the animal world. They're victims of their own success at surviving and breeding. Unfortunately for pigeons, people tend to admire that which is rare, and pigeons are plentiful. The whole pigeon-dropping situation doesn't serve the birds well, either. (It's not their fault; they are just very efficient at eliminating waste after eating.) Pigeons weren't always despised by some, though. Long ago, pigeons flew free and wild, their beautiful, iridescent feathers flashing in the sky.

They built their nests on the mountainous and rocky cliffs that lined the Mediterranean shore. Back then, as today, male and female pigeons shared parenting duty. They built nests within natural rock formations instead of on city roofs. Pigeons mate for life. "Husbands" and "wives" take turns feeding and raising the babies, two cute (but funny-looking) squabs at a time.

Thousands of years after the initial appearance of the pigeon (scientifically known as the rock dove), people captured and domesticated the bird. They found many uses for the pigeon. In early Arabia, pigeons were bred for food as well as entertainment. Families kept and selectively bred the birds for certain abilities, like rolling and tumbling in the air. A family's pigeons lived in coops and were tended to. Their droppings were beneficial to the soil and were used as fertilizer.

In India, fluffy white fantail pigeons were bred to be pleasing to the eye. They wandered in gardens and entertained children. They were also used to feed pythons.

People discovered other uses for the pigeon. Some pigeons have an incredible homing instinct, flying up to sixty miles per hour over long distances but almost always returning to their home loft. Today, the sport of pigeon racing leverages this homing ability. Usually, one bird in a mated pair is tagged with an ankle band and dropped off at a location up to hundreds of miles away. The speed and distance of the bird's flight back to the loft is calculated to declare a winner. The pigeon is not really racing but flying fast to get back to its mate or babies. Various militaries in major nation-states have used pigeons to carry messages to their allies.

Soon it was discovered that the birds were highly intelligent and able to recognize specific people, understand facial expressions, and identify shapes and objects in laboratory settings. Their physical hardiness, docile temperament, and pleasant vocalizations made them ideal subjects in psychological experiments and veterinarian schools.

This is the story of a very special racing pigeon named Woot and his equally special human best friend, Daniel.

Chapter 1 – Training Day

It was hard to breathe inside the crowded pigeon loft, where twelve-year-old Daniel Wilson and his father, Jed, scraped droppings from perches and swept dust from the cement floor. Daniel's surgical mask didn't make breathing any easier. He wore it to prevent pigeon lung, an allergy that could be so bad, people who got it usually had to go to the hospital. But despite the dust, the stifling heat, and how dark the loft was even at midday, he was happy. Sharing a love of pigeon keeping with his dad was probably the best thing in his life.

There were all kinds of purebred pigeons living in the loft. There were the fancy breeds, like Indian fantails, sporting white crowns and feathered feet. There were beautiful Jacobins, bred for chocolate-colored feathered capes. The performance breeds – rollers, tumblers, and racers – didn't look as stunning, but their athletic ability was equally impressive. The living conditions weren't great, however. It was so crowded that the birds had to compete to find a free space. Several crammed onto the triangular perches that lined the walls. A few birds splashed around in old cat litter boxes repurposed as bird baths. Others hopped on the floor and fluttered out of the way of human feet. A rusty supply bin shoved against one side of the loft contained all the necessities for pigeon keeping: seed, grit, and hay for nest building. To avoid stepping on a pigeon, Jed stubbed a toe against the bin. He cursed under his breath.

Daniel and Jed were preparing for an extremely important upcoming pigeon race: the Southwest Regional Pigeon Race. Today was training day – a practice run to see which birds were fast enough to compete in the big race.

Jed looked over at Daniel. "Which of these fertilizer machines you think we should test today?" he asked.

Daniel sneaked a glance at his father before answering. He took in his father's muscular arms and military-style hair. Jed looked tough, that was for sure.

Daniel wasn't crazy about the term "fertilizer machine." He knew his father didn't feel the same way about the birds that he did, but there was no point in making his father mad. Focus on what they had in common – that was usually Daniel's strategy for dealing with his father. "I think that blue-checked over there is looking good for it," Daniel finally said. He pointed to Woot, a robust, young adult male racer whose glossy feathers shimmered in a narrow ray of sunlight.

Jed reached into Woot's nest box and grabbed the bird. His eyes narrowed as he inspected the pigeon. "He came from winning stock, that's for sure," Jed said. "He's still healthy."

Daniel looked down at the ground. "He's my favorite," he said. "I named him Woot."

Jed raised his eyebrows and pulled the surgical mask off his face. "What do you mean, you named him? And why Woot?"

"Woot is sort of the sound he makes when I first feed him in the morning," Daniel replied. He pulled off his own mask, smiled, and imitated the "woo" cooing sound of a pigeon.

Jed was not pleased. He turned his back to Daniel as he wiped down a bird's feathers with a cloth. "Grab me that feather softener," Jed said.

Daniel complied, then scraped a few perches.

"You shouldn't get too attached to none of these birds," Jed said. "They ain't pets."

Daniel sucked in his breath and braced for an argument. "I know you think that, Dad. They're just things to you. Objects, right?"

"Well, they ain't sons or daughters," Jed responded. "You're not turning into a tree hugger on me, are you, Dan?"

Daniel decided to lighten the mood with humor. He looked at his father with mischief in his eyes. "Tree hugger!" he exclaimed. "You mean like a vegetarian? Or worse, a vegan?"

Jed laughed, then bantered back. "Hey! We don't use words like that in this household. You looking to get grounded?"

"Oh, lay off, Dad," Daniel joked.

Jed turned serious. "Look, the big race is right around the corner. We need to whip at least one or two of these birds into shape if we want to win. That's our focus. Copy that?"

Daniel was quick to agree. "One hundred percent," he said.

Jed shoved a bird out of the way with a broom before he gave the floor a final sweep. The father and son inspected several more birds in the loft before they selected nine in addition to Woot. They were eager to see how the birds would perform in the training exercise. Each bird already had a green ankle band around its right foot. Jed and Daniel entered the numbers of each ankle band one by one into a notebook. They packed two crates of five birds each and carried the crates outside.

They loaded the crates into the back of Jed's truck. Jed looked straight into Daniel's eyes. "So, here's how it's gonna work," he began. "We'll drive ten miles up the road, set 'em free, and time 'em. Let's cross our fingers we get some fast ones." They gathered the clock, calculator, and other apparatus for the trial race. Jed hoisted himself up into the driver's seat while Daniel jumped into the passenger seat of the truck. Daniel faced Jed, his expression a mixture of excitement and concern. "How many times have you done this, Dad?" he asked.

"What, train homers to race?"

"Yeah," Daniel replied.

Jed thought about it. "Well, probably at least twenty times over the years. What's on your mind?"

Daniel tried to look casual. He'd have to tread carefully here after their last conversation. "I was just wondering what happens to the slow ones," he said.

"Who cares?" Jed asked. "They ain't no use to us if they don't win."

"I know," Daniel started. "But still –"

"We'll probably just let 'em loose to fend for themselves, although some people do cull them."

Daniel tried to remember what "cull" meant. He knew it wasn't good. "Cull means –"

"Well, it means to…put an end to them, so to speak."

Daniel grew more concerned. He had a bad feeling about where the conversation was headed. He glanced at his father from the corner of his eye. "I don't know, Dad – that sounds kind of harsh."

Jed turned his head for a moment to look at Daniel. "No," he said. "It's nature. Survival of the fittest. Anyway, let's hope our birds are fast."

Jed and Daniel drove down a narrow, bumpy dirt road to a vacant stretch of land near a desert preserve. This part of Southeastern California was very hot this time of year, and nobody was around. The father and son jumped out and unloaded the two crates. Daniel stayed with the crates while Jed set up the training equipment. He waited until he was sure his father was focused on his task. Then Daniel put his face against Woot's crate and whispered softly to his favorite bird. He knew Woot wouldn't understand, but he couldn't help himself. Woot was just that cool a bird. "Good luck, buddy," Daniel whispered. "You've got to go as fast as you can."

Jed came over to the crates. Perspiration glistened on his high forehead. He wiped his hand across his brow and then rubbed both of his hands on his jeans to dry his sweaty palms. He placed his hands on the top of one crate and gestured to Daniel to take hold of the other. Jed called out instructions. "OK, now – on the count of five, whip open the top of your crate. Five, four, three, two, one!"

Jed and Daniel released the birds. Woot shot up like a rocket. The other nine followed suit. The pigeons broke off into small groups as they tried to figure out their next moves.

Out of earshot of the human pair below, the birds talked among themselves. Woot flew in a small sub-flock with two other pigeons. He looked at the birds at his side. "Look at me go!" he bragged. "I'm the fastest bird in the land. I mean in the air!" He laughed at his own silly joke.

One of the birds, a specially bred, tuxedo-colored British homing pigeon, took up his challenge. "Not if I can catch up to you, you certainly are not," she said in her clipped British accent. She moved in on Woot, but he zoomed away. The joy of freedom, of flight, was intoxicating.

Mario, a brown and gray homing pigeon, had been imported by Jed from Italy. He was out of shape and struggled to keep up. Breathless, he reached Woot. "Mama *mia*, I'm *stanco*," he said.

Woot was confused. "Stanky?" he asked.

"*Stanco*," Mario said. "It means tired."

Meanwhile, down on the ground, Jed and Daniel looked up at the sky, shielding their eyes from the glaring sun. "Come on," Jed said to Daniel. "Let's get back home. We'll clock 'em in."

They hopped back into the truck and sped off.

The pigeons were left to their own devices. Several scattered sub-flocks treaded air – almost like it was water – while they talked. Mario looked at Woot. "*Per favore*, which way do we go?"

Before Woot could answer, Tuxedo butted in. She was very proficient in technology and all the latest apps. "Seriously?" she asked. "You're lost? How can that be? You're a homing pigeon. Maybe you need a GPS? Or Google Maps?"

Woot looked at the position of the sun and frowned. He looked back at the other birds and called out. "Listen, everyone. Maybe to the humans this is just a training race, but if we don't make it home before dark, we're in big trouble. Follow me!" He sped away.

Mario looked worried. He turned to Tuxedo. "I don't see too good in the dark." Tuxedo just shrugged.

By now, Woot was half a mile ahead. He looked back and yelled, "Come on! I know the way. You can do it! Try to fly faster." He sped toward Jed's house as the other birds struggled to keep up with him. Finally, he was so far ahead of all the other pigeons that when they looked at him, all they saw was a tiny dot. Then he wasn't visible at all. In a cluster, the others followed Woot's pathway back to Jed's house, just as the sun began to set. Pink and orange clouds billowed in the sky.

Back outside the loft, Jed and Daniel sat mesmerized by the dusk ambiance. Their eager faces were rose-colored. Daniel grasped the clock and notebook tightly in his hands. His heart was pounding. He squinted at the sky, then jumped up. "Dad! Dad! I see one coming!" he exclaimed.

Woot flew at top speed but slowed down when he spotted Daniel. He put his little feet out in front, wings flapping, and landed smack-dab in the flight cage. Jed ran over to check the numbers on Woot's ankle band. "OK!" he said. "That's your bird. Number seven three five two one. Twenty-five minutes and four seconds."

"Is that good?" Daniel asked.

"Good?" Jed shouted. "It's great! Looks like your bird's a winner, Dan."

Daniel was thrilled. "Then we get to keep him?" he asked his father. "He can race in the Regionals?"

Jed shrugged his shoulders. "Yup. We'll put him on a high-performance diet, do regular bathing. But remember, it's a sport, right? He made it this time, but he's got to keep performing."

Daniel wasn't too concerned. "Sure, Dad," he said. "I understand. You taught me they're just objects."

Jed put his arm around Daniel's shoulder and gave his son a firm pat. "Why don't you go on in now," he said. "I'll be right in to make dinner."

Daniel skipped to the house. Jed looked up at the sky. He saw three more of the ten pigeons from the trial race swoop down and fly through the flight cage door into the loft. That made six who hadn't made it back yet. He looked at his watch, then glanced back at the house to make sure Daniel wasn't watching. Those other six birds were way too slow. He closed and bolted the flight cage door to lock them out. Wasn't any room in his loft for losers. The ones that didn't make it back – well, they'd just have to fend for themselves. It wasn't his problem if they starved or were eaten by hawks. That's just nature's way.

Inside the loft, the birds applauded for Woot and the other racers, who were exhausted from their harrowing training exercise. Tuxedo took the floor. "Ladies and gentlemen," she announced in her elegant voice. "Attention, please. I'm what you call beat."

Mario agreed. "Ditto," he said. "I'm not feeling so *gucci*. But I must say, we should congratulate Signore Woot. He was the best pigeon today, and that's for sure."

Woot had finally stopped panting from the exercise. He flew to the highest perch and looked down at the others. They broke into an even more rigorous round of applause and made feverish cooing noises. Woot took a bow. "And to think that the father, Jed, thinks we're just objects," he said. "Could an inanimate object fly as fast as we just did?" He zinged from perch to perch, showing off.

Woot's rival in the loft, Spirit, was a handsome, white Indian fantail pigeon, with extra feathers on his feet and on the crown of his head. Spirit was an example of a fancy, rather than performance, breed. He was bred for looks, not athletic ability. He tried to minimize Woot's accomplishment. "Sure, it could!" he said. "What about airplanes? They're objects, and they can fly."

Woot looked at him and frowned. "That's different," he said. "There are people inside doing the work. I'm the brains of my own operation. I'm going to win that big race they were talking about."

Woot's mate, Hilde, batted her big brown eyes. Hilde was a beautiful, white German owl pigeon with beige wings that looked like lace. She had a slim neck and a smooth head. "Now, I don't know, Woot, my dear," she began. "Are you sure you're ready? I know you did well this time, but you don't have to rush things –"

"Rush things?" Woot said. "I'm a racing pigeon. We're born to rush. And I have a state-of-the-art navigation system." He demonstrated by swirling his head round and round.

In the nest boxes nailed to the walls of the loft, pairs of boisterous squabs – pigeon babies, who sported fuzz and blinked their big eyes – listened to the adult birds. They laughed with glee. They were cute in an ugly sort of way.

Spirit's feathers ruffled. He was a little defensive because Woot was faster and stronger. "Some of us race only to make up for the fact that we're just not that beautiful," Spirit pointed out. "I won't mention any names, Woot, Woot." Spirit gazed at his reflection in the loft's mirror. He paced back and forth, in love with what he saw.

"Oh, yeah?" asked Woot. "Just keep admiring yourself and mind your own business."

"Hey, don't hate me because I'm beautiful," Spirit said. "I was bred to be this way." He turned his head right, then left, to find his most attractive angle.

Spirit's mate was called Sally. She was a Jacobin pigeon, another type of fancy breed. She was a Southern belle of a pigeon, with feathers that formed a chocolate-colored shawl around her neck. She hopped over to Spirit and addressed the loft. "Listen, y'all. There's a lot of money riding on this race." She turned to face Woot. "If you win, Woot, you'll score lots of points with the humans. But from my experience – in my old loft – if you lose…" She couldn't bring herself to mention the culling.

But Woot was not discouraged. "Hey, if I win, I bet the boy, Daniel, would use the prize money to renovate our digs," he said. The birds nodded in agreement and discussed all the improvements they'd get in the loft. Better chow. Straw, instead of hay, for building nests. Genuine oak nest boxes instead of veneer.

Hilde shuffled around the loft, using her wings to take mock measurements. But when she approached the flight cage door, she saw that it was locked with a dead bolt. Sally followed Hilde's gaze. They exchanged meaningful glances. A tear formed in the corner of Sally's eye. The truth about what happens to the birds who don't make it back to the loft had dawned on them. The other pigeons noticed, and the havoc in the loft was replaced with silence. Such was the reality of their existence.

To lighten the mood, one of the rolling pigeons tried to entertain the others by doing somersaults in the air. Rolling pigeons were bred to carry a genetic defect that allowed them to do circular movements that looked like somersaults. The pigeons appreciated the show. There were oohs and ahs from the spectators.

Although he was a racer and not a roller, Woot attempted a somersault too. But he couldn't do it. He merely flopped around a bit in the air and hit the ground right on his head. All the birds laughed. Hilde flew to him and nibbled his crown, charmed by her mate's antics. Woot sweetly preened her in return.

"Sweetheart, acrobatics isn't your thing," Hilde said. "But if any pigeon in California can win that race, it's you."

The birds cooed, tilting their heads in agreement and beating their wings in excitement. Woot was going to be a winner.

Chapter 2 – A Pigeon Show

Later that week, the members of the Southeastern California Pigeon Association held their quarterly meeting at a local fair. Roller coasters, a haunted house ride, and shooting galleries peppered the fairgrounds. A Ferris wheel spun in the distance. Against the backdrop of the rides and games, a makeshift barn stood unsteadily on temporary planks. The barn contained sections of different kinds of livestock: llamas, cows, horses, chickens, sheep, pigs, goats, and even an alpaca. There were a couple of horses in the barn – an Arabian and a quarter horse. A male peacock spun around, showing off his marvelous feathers. Crowds of people jammed the rows to get a good look at the animals. Except in the pigeon section. The members of the pigeon association were the only people there.

Jed, Daniel, and other club members roamed the pigeon section. Cage by cage, they examined the different types of pigeons. There was at least one pigeon representative of almost every type of fancy or performance breed: homers, rollers, tumblers, fantails, and Jacobins. It was like a pigeon beauty contest. Blue ribbons from the past year's competition were affixed to some of the cages.

Nando Carson was the president of the club. He looked a little like a crow, which was amusing, considering he was the head of a pigeon club. Nando smoothed back his weave-enhanced black hair and banged a gavel on an empty cage. "Hear ye, hear ye," he cried. "Calling to order the third annual semi-quarterly, bicentennial meeting of the Southeastern California Pigeon Association. All present say aye." The other club members chuckled at his bravado.

Clint, one of the long-timers, curled his thumbs in his overall straps and rolled his eyes. "Jeez, do we need to be this formal?" he asked. "Get a title and it goes to your head."

"I was only kidding around," Nando said. He narrowed his eye. Some of the members laughed.

Nando started the contest with the fantails.

Linda, a bleached-blond woman in her early fifties, had joined the club a couple of years earlier. Despite her pretty face, she looked a little rough-and-tumble. Her voice was hoarse from years of pack-a-day cigarette smoking. But she was kindhearted. "Here are my fantails!" she exclaimed. "They're prettier than peacocks." She placed her two best fluffy gray Indian fantails on the table. They began to strut, shaking their hips and patting the crests on their heads with their wings. The male pigeons perked up in their cages.

Nando pointed to one of Linda's birds as he consulted a checklist. He shook his head and frowned. "This one's got way too many tail feathers," he said. "See here? The tail and crown – too overdeveloped."

Knowing the humans would just hear cooing, the fantail complained to the other pigeons. "He has some nerve," she said. "With a toupee like that, he wishes he had feathers like mine!"

Nando's next stop was Spirit's cage. He lifted Spirit and inspected him closely. Nando nodded and smiled. He slapped a first prize blue ribbon on Spirit's cage. Daniel stole a glance at Jed. Jed winked back at Daniel in approval. However, Linda and Clint exchanged skeptical glances. Hmm... another winner for Jed and Daniel, just like last year.

The club members trailed behind Nando as he approached the German owl pigeon section. Only three birds were entered in this category. One bird belonged to Clint, one belonged to Linda, and the third was Woot's mate, Hilde. Nando examined Clint's bird first. "This decision's a little easier," Nando said. "See this spot on the tail? Ideally, there would be no color anywhere but on the wings." Clint stomped his foot and said, "Shoot."

Nando checked out Linda's bird next, while Linda hovered over the cage. After a few moments of silence, he left Linda's bird and moved over to Hilde's cage. He reached in and lifted her up. He turned her over to the right, then to the left. Then he went back to look at Linda's bird one last time. After what seemed like an eternity, Nando moved back over to Hilde and slapped a blue ribbon on her cage. "First place!" he said.

Woot looked over from his own cage by the other racing homers. He performed a happy pigeon dance inside.

Linda pursed her mouth tight. Really? Another win for Daniel and Jed? They had just won the fantail competition; now they placed first in the German owl category too? "Whoa – wait a minute, there," she said to Nando. "I don't get why Jed's German owl beats mine."

Nando frowned. He didn't appreciate his fairness being questioned. He stomped over to Linda's bird's cage. He reached in, grabbed her bird, and held it up to Linda's face. "Linda, this bird's just not as good a specimen as Jed's," he insisted.

Tears welled up in Linda's eyes. She had used a month's rent to purchase this purebred bird through a special website that promised that all the birds had a winning lineage.

Clint tried to console her. "It takes a while to breed a winner," he said. "Doesn't happen overnight."

"But my loft is so overcrowded," she said. "I can't just keep breeding. I keep mating my best-looking pigeons, but I'm running out of room."

"You've got to get rid of the birds that don't measure up," Nando advised. "Do it when they're young, before they can breed."

Some of the club members knew what was coming next. It was a controversial topic in the world of pigeon breeding. To cull or not to cull. Technically, there were a couple of definitions of the word. However, among pigeon breeders, it most often meant killing the birds that did not have the characteristics necessary for winning competitions or races.

"There's different ways to do it, Linda," Clint said. "You don't have to actually kill them. Just throw them out of the loft. Let them fend for themselves."

"Or you can do what I do and snap their necks," Nando said. "If you do it right quick, they don't feel pain."

At this, the pigeons in earshot shuddered. Linda looked aghast. "I don't think I can do that," she said. "It's too cruel."

Up until this point, Daniel had remained quiet. But now, sensing the reaction of the birds, he was visibly upset. "Stop it!" he cried out. "Can we please change the conversation?"

Jed shot his son a warning look. "Hey! What's the problem? You need to toughen up, Daniel. This is part of the hobby. You wanna be a winner in life, don't you?"

Daniel chewed on his bottom lip. Of course he wanted to be a winner in life, but he wanted a more humane way to succeed. He just didn't know what it was.

What had started out as a fun time now turned dark. Nando didn't want the meeting to go downhill. They had other topics to discuss. Culling was a personal decision best left to each pigeon breeder. "You know what?" he suggested. "Let's get a show from the rolling pigeons. Jed, how about you start?"

The club members murmured in agreement. Jed shrugged, then pulled out his rolling pigeon and threw the bird in the air. The bird dived gracefully down toward the table, straightened up again, and executed backflips in the air. He finished like a gymnast at the end of a routine. The club members applauded.

"Hot dang," Clint said. "You got an Olympian there, Jed."

Jed puffed up with conceit. His birds reflected him, after all.

Nando banged his gavel again. "OK, folks," he began. "Next topic: the Southwest Regional Pigeon Race. I heard the latest tally from the money pool is ten grand.

That's *mucho dinero*. Maybe I'll even enter a bird or two. Anyone else?"

Silence. Although several club members had homing pigeons that in theory could race, none were really prepared. Except for Jed and Daniel, none had birds ready to compete in such an important race. Clint and Linda looked down at their feet. Finally, Clint spoke up. "Seeing as how it's only a month away," he said, "I don't think any one of us has a bird that could fly fast enough. Except maybe Jed."

All eyes turned to Jed.

"Well, we do have one homer definitely ready to race," Jed admitted. He looked at Daniel. "It's really Daniel's bird."

"That right, Daniel?" Nando asked.

Daniel nodded and pointed to Woot. "See that large blue-check homer? We've been training him."

The members turned to look at Woot, admiring his glossy feathers and strong shape.

"It did real well," Jed bragged. He smiled at Daniel and folded his arms with pride. Daniel flushed from his father's attention.

"Yeah," Jed said. "We got it covered."

The meeting adjourned.

By eleven o'clock that night, all the people had left the fairgrounds. The full moon shone bright, adding natural light to the sky and illuminating the metal of the stilled rides. The atmosphere was magical. Tucked away in their stalls, exhausted animals slept, while others chatted about the day's events.

"I'm so hungry I could eat a horse," a Jersey cow remarked.

"Hey, I heard that," yelled the Arabian horse from his pen.

"Don't worry, dear," the cow said. "I'm a vegetarian. It was just a figure of speech. Shucks, I'm exhausted. It's bad enough I'm constantly pumped for milk, but now I have to spend two weeks cooped up in here."

"Speaking of coops," a chicken said, "this one stinks. When are they going to get around to cleaning it?"

Woot piped in from the pigeon row. "Hey, you guys, stop complaining. This is a competition. You're lucky to be here. Don't you want to make your humans proud?"

The animals cocked their heads from side to side, trying to determine the source of these challenging words. They turned toward the pigeon section.

"Are you nuts?" the chicken asked.

"Who said that?" the Jersey cow demanded. "Is that a voice from the pigeon gallery?"

The alpaca piled on, in her quaint Spanish accent: "Figures that advice would come from a pigeon. They're no good for *nada*."

"Yeah," said the Arabian horse. "Pigeons are lucky to be taken care of by people at all, seeing as they have no purpose."

Woot was indignant. "What do you mean, we have no purpose? We're smarter than most of you mammals, and smarter than many of you other birds, too."

"Really?" challenged the chicken. "Is that so? If you're so great, how come the humans won't eat your eggs?"

"And another thing," added the Jersey cow. "Bet you can't make milk. Us cows are known worldwide for our cheese." She began to list every type of cheese she could think of. "Let's see…we make brie, Swiss, Havarti, Camembert, *chèvre*…"

"Uh, excuse me," interjected a goat. "*Chèvre* is goat cheese."

"We're so beautiful," said the peacock, "the humans take care of us for free. Our only job is to walk around showing off our plumage."

"Lucky to be here?" asked the alpaca. "Did you know that I graciously donate my beautiful hair for their blankets and clothes? I also give their *niños* rides."

"*You* give rides?" asked the Arabian horse. "There's a whole industry devoted to *horse*back riding. In fact, where would humankind be without horses? Back in the Stone Age, living in caves, that's where."

"Don't forget horse racing," the quarter horse said. "Humans sure love that!"

At the mention of racing, Woot got excited. "Well, this might come as a surprise to some of you, but pigeons race too. I can fly sixty miles an hour. Bet none of you can go that fast."

Hilde turned toward the peacock. "And we're prized for *our* beauty, too," she said. She spread her wings to show off their silky, fine lace design.

The farm animals responded with stunned silence. The pigeons had made some good points. The animals had no choice but to consider this new information and reevaluate their opinion of pigeons.

"Hmm," said the Arabian horse. "I'll have to reconsider my remarks about pigeons having no purpose. To the humans, we're all pretty much what they call livestock, anyway."

"Yes," the Jersey cow agreed. "We shouldn't bicker among ourselves. Tell you what: the next time I meet a pigeon, I'll nod with respect."

Chapter 3 - Secret Talk

Daniel sat alone, quietly eating his lunch in the noisy and chaotic middle school cafeteria. The noise came from many different sources. IPhones blasted Latin hip-hop and country music. Some kids played Pokémon games. Others shouted over one another, trying to be heard but making the noise level worse. Frankie, an older boy who was repeating eighth grade, was widely known as the class bully. He was tall, with broader shoulders than the other boys'. Purple bangs covered his forehead, almost to his lashes, and contrasted with the rest of his jet-black hair. He jumped on a table. "I'm still hungry!" he cried out. "Who's got some food to give me?" He clanked a fork and spoon in hands held high over his head.

Some students laughed at the spectacle, while most shifted their eyes away from the bully. No one wanted to be a target of Frankie's attention. He repeated his demands. "Gimme some food!"

Elena, one of the popular girls, was the only person to challenge the bully. "Get real, Frankie," she said. She stared at him. "What makes you think you can act that way?"

Some of the kids chuckled.

Frankie shrugged his shoulders. "I can act this way cause no one can stop me," he answered.

He looked around. His glance landed on Daniel, sitting by himself. Frankie jumped off the table and was in front of Daniel in a flash. He grabbed Daniel's cupcake and took a bite. Some kids snickered. Others looked scared. A few of the follower types pounded the tables to egg Frankie on. One of the worst offenders, Henry, had frizzy blond hair, freckles, and a pot belly. "Careful, Frank," Henry said. "You could be eating pigeon. He and his father raise them, you know."

Frankie dropped the cupcake in a mock hot-potato motion. "You don't say. Raise them – like, what for? To eat?"

"Not sure," Henry said. "But you know, they're called rats of the sky."

Henry approached Daniel and pretended to inspect his shirt. "You got any poop on you?" he asked.

Frankie flicked an imaginary speck of bird dropping from Daniel's shoulder.

Although he felt threatened and nervous, Daniel kept his cool. He'd been through this kind of bullying before. He was his own person, and his desire to be popular with the other kids only went so far. He decided to stand up to the bullies. "You jerks don't know what you're talking about," he said.

Frankie jumped back in astonishment. "Are you calling me a jerk, you little wuss?" he yelled.

Elena stood in front of Frankie. She ran a hand through her thick black hair. "Back off, Frankie. This is so not worth getting into."

"Yeah, Frank," Henry said. "You know, Mike Tyson kept pigeons. Maybe Daniel's a boxer and we just didn't know it."

Two kids pretended to punch each other.

Daniel got up to leave, but Frankie and Henry blocked his path. "Just where do you think you're going?" Frankie challenged.

Elena positioned herself between the boys. "Don't be macho creeps," she said. "There's no reason to fight."

Just in the nick of time, before things really got out of hand, Mr. Rooney, the eighth-grade algebra teacher, entered the lunchroom. "Uh, is there a problem in here, folks?" he asked. "Lunch is over. Get back to class."

The kids scurried away.

Later that night, sleepless from the lunchtime incident, Daniel slipped out the back door and sneaked over to the pigeon loft. He moved quietly. He didn't want to wake his father. He was super quiet because he knew Jed would disapprove of a nighttime visit with the pigeons.

Daniel shrugged his shoulders as he thought about it. There was a part of Daniel that didn't care. He enjoyed the comforting feeling he got from being around the birds.

When he entered the loft, the pigeons perked up. They likely thought they'd be getting a midnight snack. A few flew right over to the closest perches. Woot, Daniel's favorite, alighted on Daniel's shoulder. Daniel smiled and stroked the bird's feathers. "Sometimes I think you pigeons are my best friends," he said under his breath.

Daniel moved about the loft with Woot still perched on his shoulder. He filled empty dishes with fresh seed and changed the water in the bathing basins. Hilde flew onto his left arm. He gently placed her in the water and added bath salts. He bathed her tenderly. "This will make your feathers smooth and soft," he whispered. She trilled happily. "You know," he said softly, "I can pinpoint all the different calls you make, but I know you guys don't really think. Dad's right. I wish it was different, but you can't think, you can't feel, you can't –"

"Talk?" Woot interrupted.

Daniel shook his head, as if to remove water from his ears. Had he just heard what he thought he'd heard?

"Oh, there's nothing wrong with your hearing," Woot said. "But now that we can understand each other, can I have a bath next? It's been a little dusty in here."

Daniel fell to the floor in shock. "What's happening?" he cried out. "Am I losing my mind? Please, Lord. Don't let me be crazy."

The other birds moved in closer to participate in the conversation.

Spirit chimed in. "You're not crazy, Daniel! You're just wiser and more clued in than most people."

"You can talk too?" Daniel gasped.

"I think you can hear all of us, dear," Hilde said. She opened her dark eyes wide. "Maybe you're a pigeon whisperer."

"Is that supposed to make me feel better?" Daniel asked. "I'm not crazy – I'm just a pigeon whisperer. Sure, that's a logical explanation."

Sally tried to make Daniel feel better about this new situation. "Honey chile, you're just sensitive," she said.

Daniel was still very anxious. He spoke out loud to feel more grounded. "Could this just be my vivid imagination?"

"Does it matter?" Woot asked.

Daniel ignored him. "I am not crazy. I am not crazy. Maybe this is all just a dream. I'll sleep here tonight, right in the corner, and when I wake up everything will be back to normal."

The pigeons weren't having any of it. They were so excited to spend more time with their favorite person. "Yay! He's staying with us tonight!" a juvenile fantail cried.

"Sleep on our side of the loft, please," Sally said.

In a playful but possessive manner, Woot took control. "No, he's my human boy," he insisted. "I can even classify him. He's in the class of mammals and the order of primates, and his genus and species are *Homo sapiens*. But I'm not sure about your breed, Daniel. Are you Anglo-Saxon? Irish-American, maybe?"

Daniel was still in shock. "I don't know how I can explain this," he muttered. "I knew pigeons were smart, but not this smart."

Woot decided a joke would ease Daniel's anxiety. "Hey, Daniel," Woot said. "Did you hear the one about why did the human cross the road?"

But Daniel was still too stunned to respond, so Spirit played along. "Why?" he asked.

"Because he couldn't fly to the other side," Woot said. The pigeons cracked up laughing.

Daniel pulled out a tarp from the supply bin, set it down, and curled up in a ball for the night. Maybe he could sleep off this crazy situation and everything would be back to normal tomorrow.

The next morning, the sun shone through a gap in the loft, right into Daniel's face. He woke up confused. "Where am I?" he thought. He sat up and looked around. "What the heck? I'm in the loft?" A growing remembrance of the previous night's events dawned on him. "Oh, yeah..." he thought. "I had that crazy dream. That dream that my birds could talk."

Woot waddled over to Daniel. His head bobbed up and down as he moved. "Good morning, Daniel!"

Daniel snapped his head around to face Woot. "Argh! It wasn't a dream!" Daniel screamed.

Woot stretched his impressive racer wings. "Not a dream, not a nightmare, but a great new reality," he said. He preened an out-of-place feather.

"Great for us," Spirit said. "Now we can get the food we want when we want it."

"Uh, I'm not so sure of that," Daniel responded. His eyes popped open. He couldn't believe he was participating in an actual conversation with his birds.

"How can you say no to us?" Spirit asked. "Especially to me. I'm so handsome."

Daniel tried to come to terms with the talking. "Maybe you are," he said, "but what will people say if they find out I can talk to you? Society is not ready for this."

Hilde said, "This can be our secret, dear. You don't need to tell any other humans about it. When they're ready, maybe they will hear us too."

Daniel considered her point. "Well, it's true – I guess I don't have to tell anyone. Parrots talk. Why not pigeons?" He pinched himself. "I'm still alive. Nobody's hurt. I might as well get used to the situation."

"That's the spirit!" Sally cried.

"You rang, my sweet?" Spirit joked. He turned toward Daniel. "Now that you can understand me better, may I make a few requests?"

"I guess so," Daniel said with hesitation.

Still trying to be lighthearted, Spirit consulted a pretend checklist. "First, I'd like to request some different kinds of peas. The Canadian peas are too large for me to swallow."

"OK," Daniel replied. "How about some of those maple peas?"

Spirit nodded. But before he could continue with additional requests, Sally jumped in. "Um, excuse me, Daniel?" she began in her smooth Southern voice. "Honey, I need a makeover. Let's start by getting me a new hairdo. Can you please clip my shawl? It gets hard to see when my feathers are in my face."

This request also seemed reasonable to Daniel. "Yeah, sure," he said. "Let me see if I can find some small scissors." He dug through the supply bin. The loft became overwhelming with activity and demands.

"We want millet! We want millet!" the younger pigeons cried in unison.

Daniel pulled out some branches of spray millet – a favorite treat of almost all pigeons – but before he could set them aside, two birds snatched the millet from his hands. They pecked at it greedily. A small group of babies circled his feet. Daniel stood on the tips of his toes to avoid stepping on the squabs.

A little brown baby pigeon cried, "I want peanuts!" A little white one asked for corn.

"C'mon, everyone. You know you need a balanced diet," Daniel said. "Millet is meant as a treat. Eat your peas." He laughed. "Now I sound like my dad."

All the demands and activity began to seem normal to Daniel. The pigeon requests and needs were what he would have expected anyway. After all, he was their caretaker. He was beginning to accept the new reality. He'd kept secrets in the past, and he could keep this one. His father didn't know that Daniel was bullied in school. What was one more secret?

Woot stepped in to help. He pursed his beak and whistled in a shrill tone. "Hey! Enough! Give Daniel some breathing room."

Woot was a bigwig in the loft, so the birds backed off. Woot hopped over to Daniel for a private chat. He sat down and crossed his wings and little legs. "What happened at school yesterday? Rough day?"

Daniel wasn't ready to talk about the lunchroom incident. He lifted Woot into the bath basin. "I think you said you wanted a bath?"

"Yes, please," Woot said. He was willing to drop the subject.

"I don't really want to talk about it," Daniel admitted.

Woot splashed around in the basin. Bathing was one of his favorite pastimes. "No problem," he said. "I'm a good listener, though."

Daniel changed his mind. Maybe Woot would understand. "Well, some of the kids at school think I'm weird because Dad and I keep you guys."

Woot frowned. "What's weird about that?"

"It's not exactly considered cool to have pigeons. It's not like being on the football team."

Woot absorbed the information. "Maybe if they got to know me better, they'd see how cool I am," he suggested. "You should bring me to school."

"I'll think about that," Daniel said. "But if you could win that big race…that would really show everyone at school that pigeons are cool. It will also make us look good to my dad." He removed Woot from the basin and placed him next to a feeding dish. "But if we're going to win, we'll need to prepare you. Here – you need to eat this high-protein mix, including your peas."

Woot didn't like peas. He turned his beak up. "No more millet?" he asked.

"Not for a while," Daniel replied. "We're putting you on a high-performance diet."

Woot looked down at his belly. "OK," he said. "I don't want to get too chunky. Say, I'm all in!"

"Great. Dad says breeding isn't everything. It's also about the preparation."

Woot cocked his head to one side. "I just thought of a rhyme. We have to bracc for the race!"

"That's a good slogan," Daniel said.

Woot flapped his wings hard, lifted off the ground, and turned in circles, like a helicopter. Daniel smiled. He could keep the secret of being a pigeon whisperer, and if Woot won the race...well, then everything would be all right. Even at school, everyone admires a winner.

The next day in the loft, Spirit and Sally sat on their eggs in a cozy nest box. Usually, each would take a turn warming the eggs while the other ate, relaxed, or gathered more nesting material. They were low on straw, so Spirit jumped out to select some nice firm pieces. He sneaked over to Woot's side of the loft, where he saw a fresh pile.

Woot caught him. "Hey, what do you think you're doing?" he asked. "Stay on your side."

"Well, we're expecting," Spirit said. "You don't have any eggs yet, so what are you hogging the straw for?"

Spirit snatched a long, thick piece. Woot grabbed the other end. Soon they played a game of tug-of-war with the piece. The straw snapped in half, causing both birds to fall back in opposite directions.

Daniel heard the commotion and entered the loft. "Hey, guys, will you please chill out? There's enough of everything to go around. I don't understand why you can't share, anyway."

Daniel had become used to his unique ability to speak to animals. He knew he had to keep it a secret, but he couldn't deny it had advantages. He just wished the birds would get along better.

Woot pointed his beak at Spirit. "He's not as cool as I am, Dan. I'm a racer and he's just a frilly fantail. At the very least, he should stay on his side of the loft."

Spirit frowned. "I may be a fantail, but I'm still pretty tough, if I do say so myself. I have a wife. We have eggs. Soon we'll have kids. Can't say the same for you."

"Not sure my dad would like it if he noticed you and Sally were paired up," Daniel said.

"Why not?" Spirit asked.

"Because you two are different breeds," Woot said. "Not a logical combination. Same situation as me and Hilde."

The other mated pairs in the loft nodded in understanding. Spirit was a fantail and Sally was a Jacobin. Even though they were both in the fancy pigeon category, they were technically different breeds. It was a sad fact of their existence that the humans controlled everything. Not just food and lodging, but who married whom. Daniel was one of those rare humans who saw them as individuals.

Sally looked at Woot. "That's right, Woot. When are you and Hilde going to have babies?"

Woot glanced at Hilde and then looked away. "I don't know," he said. "Maybe after the race –"

Hilde didn't want Woot to feel bad. She lit up. "That's OK, Woot. Let's just focus on the race for now. We have our whole lives ahead of us."

Woot smiled. Hilde was the best pigeon mate a racing homer could ask for. Pigeons might have a lot of needs, but they were usually good sports. He turned to face Daniel. "I know we can be a lot of work," Woot said. "Poop everywhere – we make a mess. Most of us are not neat freaks."

"The cleanup doesn't bother me," Daniel said. "It's just that since I take care of you and you don't want for anything, why can't you all just get along? You seem so territorial. Sometimes you remind me of…people."

"Now, there's no reason to insult us!" Spirit replied.

"We're sorry, Daniel," Hilde said. "You don't need to see all our flaws."

"We also have many virtues," Woot said. "Hey, guys. Should we let Daniel in on the secret rhyme of pigeons?" The birds nodded.

"I'll tell it," Spirit said.

"No, really," Woot insisted. "I think he needs to hear it from me. OK, Dan, here it goes." Woot pumped out the rhyme in a hip-hop rhythm: "A pigeon's virtues are great, I'd like to state. I'll share them now, why make you wait? Intelligence, loyalty, only one mate. But the most impressive: We navigate. Distance near or far, we can create / a pathway home to our lofty gates. So next time you see one, don't loathe or hate. A new friend for life, so affectionate."

Everyone clapped.

"Wow. That's the secret pigeon rhyme?" Daniel asked.

"The very one," Woot said.

Chapter 4 –
Woot Scores in Science Class

Daniel usually looked forward to science class. Science and math were his two favorite subjects and he was widely known for his ability. The main topic in this week's class was evolution. Daniel found this especially fascinating. The science teacher was Mr. Price. While some said Mr. Price was a bit of a nerd, Daniel thought he was smart, as most nerds are. Daniel had once heard the expression "Nerds rule the world." Boy, it would be great if that were true.

Mr. Price had suggested Daniel bring a pigeon to class sometime to demonstrate the principles of evolution. Apparently, Darwin himself raised pigeons. So today was the day. Unfortunately, the kids were unruly, and Frankie, the bully, was also in this class. While Mr. Price was kind as well as smart, he didn't always control the class very well. Even now that class was about to start, some kids sat on their desks, gossiping and playing on their iPhones.

To get the kids' attention, Mr. Price stood up and clapped his hands. Sweat dripped down the temples of his mahogany-colored face. He took off his glasses and mopped his brow with the handkerchief he kept in his shirt pocket. "Class, please calm down! On your laptops, pull up the website using the link I sent you and we'll discuss Charles Darwin and the theory of evolution by natural selection. Now, who can explain the theory?"

Silence.

"Did anyone read the homework assignment?"

"I read it," Elena replied.

"Great. In your own words, please explain it to us."

"Well," Elena began, "it means that some…uh… qualities, I guess you'd say, come from something called genes. These qualities give some members of a…uh… species an edge in surviving or in finding a mate. The ones who do get to pass down these qualities or genes to future generations."

Mr. Price raised his eyebrows and tilted his head in approval. "That's pretty close. Pretty good," he said. He smiled his encouragement at Elena. "Please proceed."

But before Elena could continue, Frankie jumped from his chair and flexed his biceps. "I must have good genes," he bragged, "'because I can get as many mates as I want."

Some kids laughed, but Elena rolled her eyes and said, "I think the most important genes for attracting mates have to do with intelligence."

"Oohs" and "ahs" emerged from the class at her put-down.

Mr. Price struggled to get them back on track. He cleared his throat. "I'd also like to point out another aspect of the theory. Throughout evolutionary history, there has been a tension between two strategies for a species' survival: cooperation and aggression. Can anyone elaborate?"

Elena again was the only one to respond. "Um, maybe it means that in both the animal kingdom and the human kingdom sometimes the males fight over stuff. Like mates or food?"

Mr. Price said, "Yes, and –"

"And at other times if you pull together, you'd do better at building a house, or even doing something like hunting?" Elena asked.

"Good!" Mr. Price exclaimed. "So, we learned that cooperation can get us further than working on our own."

"Say, Mr. Price?" Elena asked.

"Yes, Elena?"

"What about God?"

"What about God?" Mr. Price replied.

"Well, my mother said evolutionary theory goes against God."

"I don't think that has to be the case, Elena," Mr. Price said. "Some would say the two views are actually consistent. Would you like to take a stab at reconciling the two?"

Elena paused as she considered the puzzle. "Well, maybe the aggression part of human nature is what the Bible would say is evil and the cooperation part is good."

"Maybe," Mr. Price said. "The answers to these questions are very personal and I think each of us has to search inside for the answers. But speaking of cooperation, it just so happens that we have a special surprise today. Daniel Wilson has brought his homing pigeon to class to help drive home some points about natural selection. Dan?"

Daniel looked around at his classmates and then at Mr. Price. "Thanks," Daniel began. "The topic of pigeons came up at lunch the other day, so I thought you'd like to meet one." He opened his pet carrier and positioned Woot on his open hand for the class to view. "This is a blue-checked homing pigeon. You can see how his wing span is designed for maximum speed and height." He gently pulled Woot's wing to demonstrate the point.

Mr. Price continued. "Darwin theorized that all modern pigeons descended from the original wild rock dove, *Columba Livia*," he said.

The class was interested and even a little bit charmed. Frankie, noticing that the class was engaged, tried to make a joke. "See, they weren't even American," he yelled. "They came from Colombia."

No one laughed. Daniel decided to take the high ground and ignored the bully. "Pigeons are monogamous," Daniel continued. "That means they mate for life. They enjoy bathing. They have excellent day vision, so they can pick out the seeds and vegetables that are safe to eat."

"This is boring," Frankie said.

Daniel tried to tune him out. "Back to the points Mr. Price made earlier. Sometimes the pigeons in our loft argue – I mean, uh, fight for the best perch. But when they get scared, if they see a hawk or something, they huddle together for protection."

The class was rapt with attention. But suddenly, Frankie rushed to the front of the room. "Give me that bird!" he cried. Before anyone could stop him, he grabbed Woot and threw him out the window.

The students – and Mr. Price – gasped. At first, everyone was too stunned to act.

Then Elena screamed at Frankie. "What did you do that for?"

Before Frankie or anyone else could say a word, in a flash, Woot flew straight back through the window and landed on Frankie's shoulder. The kids clapped and shouted with delight.

"That's what I'm talking about," Daniel said. "That's part of the homing instinct. My pigeon can navigate and come back to wherever he was launched."

Frankie glanced at his shoulder. "Ew, he just pooped on me!"

The kids laughed.

Silently, Woot flew back into his pet carrier.

"Don't worry," Elena joked to Frankie. "It's supposed to be good luck. With your attitude, you're going to need it."

When school let out for the day, Daniel headed home with Woot in the carrier. He saw Elena and Henry outside. They stood in the middle of a group of cool kids. Elena noticed Daniel. She turned to her group, "Hey, you guys," she said. "I'll catch up with you later." She ran toward Daniel. "Daniel! Wait up."

Henry yelled back at her. "What? You're going to hang out with the lame pigeon nerd?"

Elena ignored him as she caught up with Daniel.

"Hey," Daniel said.

"Hey," Elena said back. She gestured at the pet carrier. "How's your pigeon doing? What did you say his name was?"

"Woot," Daniel replied. "He's doing OK."

Elena peeked inside the carrier and greeted Woot. "Hi, Woot," she said. "You're so sweet."

Woot turned to Daniel and whispered. "Psst. Daniel. She's real nice. You should invite her over."

Of course, all Elena heard was a cooing sound. "Wow, he's really precious," she said. "I love the sounds he makes."

"Thanks," Daniel said.

Elena looked down at her feet. "Look, I just wanted to say that you shouldn't let Frankie get to you. He's not a bad person."

Daniel raised his eyebrows. "Yeah? Did you know he posted a cartoon of a dead pigeon on his Facebook page and tagged me?"

"Yeah," Elena said. "I heard about that. That was stupid of him." She paused. "I don't know exactly what to say, Daniel, except that I think you're really smart in science. And that's pretty cool." She started to walk away.

"Hey, Elena," Daniel called.

She looked back. "Yeah?"

"If you're interested and you think you might like pigeons, you could come by the loft some time. Or maybe even to one of the pigeon club meetings."

Elena smiled. "I'd like that. Bye, Woot!"

Chapter 5 – Taking The High Road

Elena may have defended Frankie, but it wasn't clear at all that he was a good person. Sometimes it's hard to tell if someone is just plain mean because of his personality, or if that person has something going on in his life to make him act a certain way. In Frankie's case, no one knew that his home life was very challenging.

While Elena and Daniel were chatting, Frankie walked home alone. For Frankie, home was a rundown shack of a house on the wrong side of the railroad tracks.

He opened the front door to the house. His mother, Karla Collins, almost bumped into him. She looked frazzled. Her hair was messy, and she slouched, trying to balance Frankie's infant half-brother on her left hip while holding the hand of a toddler in her right hand. She pretty much pounced on Frankie. "Where you been?" she asked. "I'm late for work and I need you to watch the kids."

"OK, chill out," Frankie growled back. "I'm here." He moved toward the refrigerator. "I need a snack first. I'm starving."

For a split second, his mother's face wore a guilty expression. Then it was gone. "There's nothing for a snack. I haven't been able to get to the supermarket since I had to take care of these kids. I'll try to bring dinner back on my way home."

"But you don't get off work until nine!" Frankie said, alarmed. "What am I supposed to eat until then?"

Vexed, Karla shook her head. "I don't know. Ray is supposed to stop by later. Maybe you can ask him to go out and get food if you can't wait till I get back."

At the mention of Karla's boyfriend, Ray, Frankie got angrier. "As though that jerk would ever do a favor for someone else," he snorted.

"Don't open your mouth to me!" Karla said. She headed toward the door. "I'm going. See you tonight." She handed him his baby brother and bounded out the door.

Frankie carried the infant in the crook of his arm while he searched the refrigerator for something to eat. It was empty, except for a head of lettuce, a jar of baby formula, some moldy cheese, and a six-pack of Michelob Light.

He moved to a small adjoining room that barely passed as a living space and threw an old newspaper off the beat-up couch before he plopped down. The newspaper joined the others that were strewn all over the floor. He strapped the infant into the car seat next to him on the couch. The toddler sat down on his other side. Frankie reached for the remote and clicked through the channels. Dang it! He was hungry! He could hear his own stomach growling.

Thirty minutes later, the front door opened, and Ray charged inside. Ray was tall but slightly built, with acne scars on his face and thin mousy brown hair. He looked over at Frankie. "Yo, man, what's up?"

Frankie didn't answer.

"I asked you a question. Didn't you hear me?" Ray asked.

"No," Frankie lied. "I was focused on the TV."

Ray didn't fall for it. "When I talk to you, you better answer immediately."

Frankie stared at the TV.

"No wonder you were held back in school. You're such a loser." Ray wouldn't let it go.

Frankie stood up. He was almost as tall as Ray and built bigger. He snarled, "You're not my father. You can't talk to me like that."

In a flash, they were in each other's faces. Spit ran from the corner of Frankie's mouth. But Ray gave it right back to him.

"Thank God for that," he said. "I'd be ashamed if you were my son." Ray glanced at the toddler, then back at Frankie. "I won't let your brother turn out like you."

"Oh, big man with a big mouth. You don't even pay rent here!"

Ray took a deep breath. Rather than escalate the verbal argument into a physical one, he decided to leave. But not without giving Frankie one last dig. "It's a good thing your mother's so pretty," he said. "Otherwise I'd never put up with this bull." He bolted out the door and slammed it shut behind him.

But just before the door closed, a skinny German shepherd mix slipped inside. It was the family dog, who barely got any attention. The dog sniffed the floor, looking for food. He barked loudly at Frankie.

"Shut up!" Frankie snapped. "I got nothing to feed you."

The dog whimpered. His sad state made Frankie feel even worse. "What do you expect me to do?" he asked the mutt. "There's nothing to eat, even for me."

The dog moved closer to Frankie. Frankie shoved him away with his foot. "Get off me, you stupid mutt," he said. The dog slinked away. Frankie wiped tears from his eyes.

Later that night, Daniel hung out in the loft with the pigeons while he did his homework. Ever since he'd learned he could talk to the pigeons, he had enjoyed his time with them even more. He sat cross-legged in a corner with his laptop balanced on his legs. The light from the overhead lamp contrasted cozily with the blackness outside. The flashlight app on Daniel's iPhone illuminated his laptop screen. While he concentrated, Woot perched on Daniel's shoulder and looked down at the laptop. "Whatcha reading?" he asked.

"I'm reading about you guys, pigeons, and how you all evolved."

Woot cocked his head to one side. "What does 'evolved' mean, Daniel?"

Daniel sighed. "It's a little hard to explain, but basically it means how you and other pigeons got to be the way you are today."

"You mean all the different breeds?"

Daniel nodded. "That's part of it."

"I've noticed that humans come in different shapes and colors too," Woot said. "So, there must be different breeds of humans."

Daniel paused to consider this idea. "When it comes to humans we call it races or ethnic groups, not breeds. But you make a good point. It's kind of superficial because there's only one species. Human."

"Just like all pigeons are one species?" Woot asked.

"Yes," Daniel responded. But before he could continue to explain, his laptop pinged with an Instagram notification. "Oh no!" Daniel shouted. He clicked on his Instagram account to find that he was tagged in an image of a building with pigeons crowded on the roof. Pigeon droppings covered the walls. The hashtag read: "#DanielWilson'sHouse."

"What's wrong?" Woot asked.

"It's Frankie Collins again," Daniel replied.

Woot flew to Daniel's right shoulder and viewed the photo. "I got to tell you, Daniel, I don't like that guy."

Hilde flew over and landed on Daniel's leg. "What can we do?" she asked.

Spirit lit up. "Let's get even!" he cried. He flew to Daniel's right shoulder, and then hopped down to his lap. He used his beak to type on Daniel's keyboard.

Sally asked, "What are you writing? What's it say?"

"It says, 'Frankie Collins is a loser,'" Spirit said. "We can send it out to the whole school."

"Not so fast," Woot said. "I have a better idea. Do this for me, Dan. Google 'Cher Ami.'"

Daniel nodded and started typing.

"Who's Cher Ami?" Spirit asked.

"You don't know who Cher Ami is?" Woot asked. "Did you flunk pigeon history?"

Spirit shrugged. "Yeah, I was always better in math."

Spirit, Woot, Hilde, and Sally gathered on spots along Daniel's shoulders and arms and gazed at the laptop screen. An image of the famous war hero pigeon, Cher

Ami, appeared with a caption: "U.S. Army Signal Corps, World War I. She was the hero of the 77th Infantry Division." Daniel cut and pasted the image. He added the hashtag: "#PigeonsRock." After one last look, he posted it to his Instagram account. All the kids in school followed each other so he knew all his classmates would see it. The tension in the loft subsided.

Hilde sighed. "A female war hero. The bravest pigeon ever."

"Yes," Sally added. "She was ahead of her time."

Hilde and Sally pointed their wings at each other in a mock gun salute. They laughed. The rest of the birds clapped their wings at the spectacle.

The next week Jed invited his friends from the pigeon club to meet on the patio outside his loft. They munched on junk food and drank beer. Many brought their pigeons to the meeting. The birds were cooped up in small cages stacked in rows several feet away from the patio table.

Nando raised his eyebrows at Jed. "So, did you make a final decision about which birds you'll enter in the race?" he asked.

Before Jed could answer, Daniel and Elena came out of the house and joined the crew. Nando was surprised to see Daniel with a friend. He'd never brought anyone around the pigeons before. Nando smiled at Elena. "Who are you?"

Daniel looked down at his feet. He was slightly embarrassed, but he knew he had to introduce Elena. "Hey, everyone. This is Elena. Elena Martinez."

Elena looked around with surprise. "Wow," she said. "You sure do have a lot of pigeons here."

Jed and his friends looked at each other. Was Elena's remark a compliment or an insult? Linda patted her hands on the empty seats on either side of her. "Pull up a seat, you two," she said. "Join us for the conversation." She turned toward Elena. "Nice to meet you, Elena. You came out just in time to hear about the big race. The Southwest Regional."

Elena looked puzzled.

"We need to decide which birds to enter," Nando explained. "There'll be folks from a lot of western states. Utah, Arizona, Nevada, maybe even New Mexico. I'm going to enter two birds. There's a sweet pot of money at the end of the rainbow."

"I'll enter the three birds that did decent in training," Jed said, "but I'm pretty pumped about just one." He glanced at the loft, in Woot's direction. "My favorite for this race is Daniel's bird. It did great during training."

Elena looked at Daniel. "Isn't that Woot?" she asked.

Jed frowned. "Now you got your friends naming the birds, too?" he asked.

Daniel bit his lower lip. He didn't want to argue with his father in front of Elena, but why couldn't he understand that not everyone saw animals as objects? He took a deep breath. The night before Woot had showed him that taking the high road paid off, so that's what Daniel decided to do again. "Yeah, Dad. I brought Woot to class the other day."

"I bet he got better grades than some of the kids at that school," Clint joked.

Nando stole a glance at Woot. "If you got three contenders, Jed, you might as well enter them all. Nothing to lose but the entry fee."

"That's what I'm thinking," Jed said.

"If some birds don't make it back, you can always breed more. Nature's way of improving the bloodline, right?" Nando pointed out.

Some of the club members nodded their agreement.

"And then you can do better next year," Clint said.

"I never realized pigeons could race," Elena said. "I thought that was only for horses, or greyhounds."

"Let me explain it to you," Jed said. "The way it works is that we take the male or female of a mated pair who have a couple of eggs or squabs. The pigeon tries to get back to its mate as fast as it can. It's called a widow or widower strategy."

Elena was horrified. "You mean the pigeon is trying to get back to its family?"

Nando snorted. Jed slapped his hands on his thighs and let out a laugh.

Nando leaned over to Jed and whispered, "Looks like another bleeding heart coming around. You'll want to watch that."

"We'll straighten her out," Jed whispered back. He turned toward Elena. "So that's how racing works, but most of us are also into breeding the fancies. That's good competition too."

Elena raised her eyebrows.

Clint explained. "Racing, rolling and tumbling are what's called performance breeding. We swap those kinds of pigeons at these get-togethers, too."

Jed turned to Nando. "Nando, that reminds me. That Jacobin you had that won first place at the fair – you still got any of its eggs or squeakers?"

"I do," Nando said. "You want to make a trade? I'd love one of your German owls. You had some white ones with beige wings –"

"Done and done!" Jed said. "I've got a female I don't really need anymore. If you want her, I'll swap her for one of your Jacobin eggs."

Nando and Jed high-fived on the swap.

Jed went inside the loft and came back with Hilde. He handed the bird to Elena to check out.

"Ooh, she's beautiful," Elena gushed.

Daniel jumped up. Hilde was Woot's mate! He couldn't let his father trade her.

Pigeon coos of protest erupted from the loft. There was no way Daniel would let Hilde go with Nando. He had to think fast. "Uh, Dad. You can't trade that bird," he said.

"Why not?" Jed asked.

Daniel struggled to come up with an excuse. He knew pointing out that Hilde was married to Woot would never fly. Maybe he could say he wanted to keep Hilde to try to breed her with Woot as an experiment. At least that wouldn't make him look soft. "Because I was going to breed her to a blue-checked to see what happens."

"That's a terrible idea," Jed responded. "That kind of mix makes no sense."

Elena sensed Daniel's plight. "You know what? Do you think *I* could have her? I'll even pay you for her," she said.

"You want to keep the bird as a pet?" Jed asked.

"Uh, yeah," Elena said. "We're real animal people at my house. My mom has a cockatiel and two dogs." Elena stared at Daniel. "Do you think you can keep her in your loft for a while, though? I'll need time to buy supplies and get set up."

Jed didn't want to turn down Daniel's new friend. Besides, it was nice to get more young people involved in the hobby. He looked at Nando. "Nando, that OK with you? We can do a trade another time."

"Shoot," Nando said, "it's not that big a deal. What's one bird versus another? Let the girl have it."

"You know that old saying about the size of a bird brain," Clint said.

Daniel couldn't resist the opportunity to set the record straight. "Birds may have smaller brains than mammals, but they have a higher density of neurons in those brains," he said.

Elena looked at Daniel with admiration. "You are so good at science!"

Daniel beamed.

Chapter 6 – Race Day

The Southwest Regional Pigeon Race was famous to pigeon fanciers around the country. It was like the Olympics of pigeon racing. And to the pigeon fanciers who lived in the Southwest, it was the event they trained for all year. Jed and Daniel were no exception. Race day was finally here!

It was the crack of dawn. A refurbished Mack truck, already loaded with caged birds, lumbered down a dirt road. On the side of the truck, a sign read "Southern California." This truck was one of many headed toward the race release point. This year, as in years past, the venue was in the tristate area, where California, Arizona and Nevada bordered each other. The roaring Colorado River was close by.

On its way to the tristate area release point, the Southern California truck made stops at several rural properties. At each stop, pigeon owners loaded their racers onto the truck. After a couple of hours, the truck finally pulled up to Jed and Daniel's house. Nando was there, too, with his one racing pigeon. All three humans wore the same focused expression. Jed placed an electronic ring around Woot's ankle, then on Tuxedo's ankle, and finally on Mario's. With quick, efficient, and confident movements, he entered each bird's numbers into a computer. "You see how it's done, Dan?" he asked his son. "It's like a training exercise, but more scientific. You've got to synchronize the ankle band with the computer. The computer will calculate the time over distance at the end of the race. That's how the winner is determined."

Daniel nodded, concentrating so he could learn. Nando stepped over to help Jed and Daniel load the cages onto the Mack truck. They let each cage down gently. When they were finished, the two men and the boy hopped into Jed's pickup truck and followed the Mack truck to the release point.

The same process was occurring at different locations across the Southwest. Racing pigeon club members proudly loaded their cages filled with racers onto their own state trucks. Some states required their club members to meet at a specific location. For example, in Nevada, the designated pick-up point was in beautiful Red Rock Canyon. In Arizona, the state pigeon club members met at a huge parking lot in downtown Tucson. One man, sporting a cowboy hat, stood surrounded by his posse of club members. He examined his favorite bird's electronic ankle band before loading him onto the truck. Then he, too, entered the numbers into a computer.

For the Utah crew, the gathering place was outside a desert wash. A crowd cheered for their local clubs as the Utah truck pulled away.

Regardless of the state, those who were interested enough to make the trip could drive to the tristate area and watch the spectacle. Jed, Daniel and Nando were among those who went to the release point.

Anticipation filled the air. An emcee spoke to the crowd through a bullhorn. "OK, everyone," he began. "Get into your ready positions."

The drivers and their assistants stood at their state trucks. For the folks who didn't have assistants, the racing organization provided staff to help release the birds. In the Southern California truck, Jed, Nando, and Daniel hovered over their cages, poised for the release. Daniel's arm muscles tensed. His heart pounded with excitement. He knew Woot was ready!

The race emcee started the countdown. "On the count of five: five, four, three, two, one!"

All the pigeon people flung their cages open. Hundreds of birds flew into the air. Their wings painted the desert sky with color, and the sound of wings fluttering was like music to human ears.

For the birds, it was chaos.

Woot and Tuxedo flew next to each other. Mario was nowhere to be seen.

A stranger, a multicolored racing pigeon, cried out, "Help! Help! Where am I? I don't recognize this place!"

A sleek white racing pigeon from Arizona shouted with glee. "Whee! Look at me. I'm soaring!"

Tuxedo turned toward Woot. "We're a lot farther away than the last time we flew together. I'm a bit concerned."

Woot said, "I know. But I think I've got it covered. Follow me."

"Can I come along?" the scared multicolored racing pigeon asked.

Tuxedo looked confused. "Aren't you from Utah?" she asked. "We're going in different directions."

The white racing pigeon flew alongside. "I'm from Arizona, but I'm not going back to that smelly hole in the ground they call a pigeon coop," she said.

"You don't know what you're talking about," Tuxedo replied. "What are you going to do for food? For water? Did you think about that?"

The white pigeon tilted her head from one side to the other. It seemed most of these birds were not well prepared, after all. It was clear the birds needed a leader. Woot knew he had to take charge. The lives of these birds depended upon him. He launched his instructions. "Listen up, everyone," he began. "You birds from Utah need to go north. The birds from Arizona need to go south. Those from Nevada head southeast, and California birds, follow me. We're mostly heading west."

The pigeons broke apart into separate flocks, flying in the different directions. Woot flew in front of the California flock. "Speed is of the essence," he said. "It's a long way off. It's much safer to fly while it's still light out." With that, he zoomed away at top speed as the others struggled to follow. But the California birds just couldn't keep up with him, no matter how hard they flapped their wings. Soon Woot was flying alone.

At first, Woot flew briskly in the correct direction to Daniel and Jed's loft. He was off to a good start. But his flight path included the Sonoran Desert in Arizona, and this time of year was monsoon season. Monsoons in Arizona consist of torrential rain storms. Storms that could be so powerful that they often created flash flooding.

As bad luck would have it, a storm was brewing. Bolts of lightning flashed. Thunder boomed. A massive downpour soaked Woot's feathers until they were so heavy, they weighed him down to the ground. Then a forceful gust of wind hit his little body and blew him back up in a zigzag motion – first in one direction, then another. It was a haboob, a kind of dust storm seen only in the desert. He blinked his eyes to clear his vision from the dust. Another gust of rain hit him in his little face. He was knocked back down to the ground. That was the last straw. He would have to wait out the storm before going any farther. He looked around for shelter. The best he could find was a thick palo verde tree. He crawled along the ground with his wings over his head like an umbrella until he reached the bottom of the tree. He stayed there, hoping to wait out the storm.

Later that evening, saguaro, prickly pear, and cholla cacti glistened in the moonlight. The desert was always so beautiful after a rain storm. The earthy and delicious smell of creosote perfumed the air. Woot stood up and shook his head. He fluttered his feathers. He joked to himself to cut back on his fear. "Holy moly! I know I need a shower, but this is ridiculous. Where am I? Could I be lost? Is that even possible?"

He scanned the terrain, looking for a place to roost for the night. Pigeons don't like to be too low to the ground at dark. It makes them vulnerable to predators. He jumped up to a higher branch of the palo verde tree. He perched on the branch and hugged his little body with his wings. He had never been truly alone before. "I want to go home," he thought. But it wasn't happening that night. He recited part of the pigeon rhyme aloud to feel better. "Distance near or far, we can create / a pathway home to our lofty gates." He flew to an even higher branch for safety. The rain had stopped, but the wind was still gusting. The branches of the palo verde tree swayed vigorously. Woot stared out into the night with big round eyes.

Meanwhile, other birds had fared better during the race. High up in the sky, a flock of four fluttered their wings in their final descent, just in time for sunset. Some pigeons had even made their way back to their lofts. At an old wood loft in Nevada, two birds made a smooth landing into their flight cage. A man – Mr. Jones – removed the first bird's electronic ankle band and entered the numbers into a computer. The computer screen showed the four fastest birds of the race. They were listed by their ID numbers, the owners' last names, and their states:

"28131 Jones, Nevada; 89310 Claymont, California; 19290 Torres, Arizona; 31382 Dinkers, California."

Mr. Jones jumped and yelled with joy at winning.

Outside his loft, Jed awaited the return of his three birds. His facial muscles were stiff with tension. He looked up at the sky. Two birds came into view. It was Tuxedo and Mario. Jed opened the flight cage of the loft and the birds crash-landed inside. Jed followed the birds inside, grabbed their feet, and entered the numbers on their ankle bands into his computer. He checked the screen and saw that neither bird had won. He frowned and pursed his mouth in disappointment. Daniel ran out of the house. "Dad, Dad! They're back?" he yelled.

"Yeah, but so what?" Jed replied. "They were slower than molasses."

Daniel ran into the loft, whipping his head around. "I only see two! Where's Woot?"

Jed turned to face him. "Stop it!" he demanded. "I told you not to name those dang birds. Your favorite hasn't even made it back yet. Maybe he won't make it back at all."

Daniel tried to keep his composure as he held back tears. "Don't say that. He was the fastest. The strongest."

"Wake-up call," Jed said. "He wasn't. I was counting on that prize money. Guess I'll have to take some extra shifts at the plant after all."

Daniel walked out of the loft. He screwed up his face and gazed at the sky. Stars twinkled in the dimming light. He turned on his heels and silently walked into the house. He glanced at the sky one last time before closing the door. "Woot, where are you?" he wondered.

Chapter 7 – Lost In Arizona

At daybreak, Woot was still perched on a high branch of the palo verde tree. He was completely unfamiliar with this patch of the Sonoran Desert. He thought it was beautiful though. The sunshine poured over the landscape and lifted his spirits. Other birds chirped. Woot flew from his branch to the ground and shook his feathers. "Phew!" he thought to himself. "I made it through the night." He spotted a cactus wren eating some seeds in the hole of a saguaro cactus. "Hey, you over there," Woot called.

The cactus wren ignored him.

"You, cactus wren," he persisted. "I'm talking to you. Please answer me."

"Oh, I'm sorry," the cactus wren said with sarcasm. "I should have just dropped what I was doing to converse with you. What matter that I'm eating my breakfast?"

"Look, I'm sorry to bother you, but I'm lost and I was hoping you could give me directions."

The cactus wren laughed. "That's rich," he said. "A homing pigeon wants directions from a wren. That's a hoot."

Nearby, Charlie, a barn owl, had been sleeping in another cactus. He overheard the conversation and was startled by the word "hoot." He took off his spectacles and rubbed his eyes. "Did someone call me?" he asked.

"Relax, Charlie," the cactus wren said. "This pigeon here is lost."

"Oh no!" Charlie exclaimed. He looked Woot over. "Well, we don't see too many of your kind here. Where are you from?"

"I'm from Blythe, California," Woot said. "I need to get back to my family."

Charlie reached into the cactus hole and pulled out an atlas. "Let's see," he said as he flipped through the pages. "Blythe, Blythe. Ah! OK, here it is. Latitude three three point six one seven eight north. Longitude: minus one fourteen point five eight eight three west."

Woot didn't know if he should be grateful or exasperated. He could try to set his internal navigation by these coordinates, but that's not usually how he found his way back. He decided to be gracious. "Say, thanks for that," he said. "That's very helpful." He squinted his eyes and concentrated on the coordinates. Maybe he could program his brain. "I'm off, you guys," he said. "Thanks again for your help." With that, he soared high up into the sky with a renewed sense of purpose.

"Well, that's more like it," he thought to himself as he flew. "Things are looking up." His stomach growled. "Could use a bite to eat though." He scanned the terrain below, looking for food. Soon he spotted a flowering ironwood tree. Beige pods were scattered across the ground where the tree was rooted. He dived in the direction of the tree, but he was so focused on the iron pods that he didn't see a power line in the way. He hit the power line head-on. His feathers stood on end from the shock. He dropped to the ground, hopping on one foot. He wasn't badly hurt –

just dazed. He made his way to the ironwood tree. He nibbled the pods. "A little bland. Could use some salt," he joked to himself.

Overhead, Lucy, a red-tailed hawk, was also looking for food. She was magnificent. Her beauty was matched by her confidence. She flew like she owned the sky. She spied Woot below. She mumbled to herself, "Oh, goodie. My dinner is eating its dinner. Now, Lucy, don't mess this up. Keep letting them slip away and you'll starve to death. Quiet, quiet. Now go." She swooped down in Woot's direction, but he heard her before she could grab him. An ironwood pod dropped from his beak as he lifted off the ground. Lucy gave chase.

Woot was terrified. He'd heard lots of bad things about hawks, but he'd never encountered one before in the safety of Jed's loft. He soared higher, making sure to avoid the power lines. He could do this! He was a racing pigeon, after all. But, while he had a good lead, Lucy was also very fast.

"Wait, wait!" Lucy cried. "Why are you flying away from me? I just want to talk to you. You know, make some new friends. Maybe have dinner?"

Woot shouted back at her. "Don't take this the wrong way, but I've heard stories about hawks. You're known to say, 'Oh, you don't need to bring anything to dinner... just yourself.' No thanks!"

Lucy closed in on Woot, narrowing the distance between them. Woot was getting winded. It was hard to breathe. Lucy drew closer, closer, and then wham! She nipped his behind. He struggled free, leaving her holding a tail feather in her beak. She spat it out. "Ugh," she thought. "The tail feathers are the worst."

Woot had gotten away for the moment, but what now? He saw a hole in a huge saguaro cactus up ahead. He flew into the hole and hid inside the hollow of the cactus. But she had seen him. She followed right through the same hole. He flew higher inside the cactus and escaped through another hole, higher up. Being quite a bit larger, Lucy had trouble getting out of the higher hole. She managed to squeeze her way out but was pricked by cactus needles in the process. "What is this, acupuncture?" she asked herself, vexed. She gave chase again. She was hungry and determined to get her prey.

Woot flew to an even higher elevation. Trying to keep his spirits and motivation up, he joked to himself. He pretended to be an air traffic controller. "This is Captain Woot. I'm facing some congestion in the area. Is it safe to go lower?" He made a dive down, then up.

After what seemed like an eternity, high-rise buildings came into view. It was downtown Phoenix, Arizona, in the near distance. Woot spotted what looked to be an abandoned building. He flew through the jagged hole of a broken window. Lucy tried to follow him, but she just couldn't fit through the window without cutting herself. She finally gave up and flew away. Cactus needles were one thing. Getting cut up from glass was quite another.

"And this guy's a little too fast. There's gotta be some easier prey," she thought.

Woot paused to catch his breath. Still panting, he looked around the dimly lit room. He couldn't make out any images, but someone spoke to him in the dark. "Who's there?" a rough voice called out. "Don't ya believe in knocking?"

As Woot adjusted his eyes to the dark, a flock of feral city pigeons came into view. The leader, Hipster Pigeon, spoke in a New York accent. "Say, fella, are you OK?" he asked.

Before Woot could respond, a dainty little female street pigeon whistled in his direction. "Check out this beautiful specimen of *Columba Livia*," she said, referring to Woot.

The pigeons circled Woot. He was a little nervous. He knew pigeons could be territorial, but they weren't usually aggressive. It was certainly a safer situation than dealing with a hawk.

Exhausted, Woot said, "Hello, everyone. I didn't mean to intrude. It's been a rough couple of days. Can you spare something to eat and drink?"

A scrawny, teenaged pigeon answered. "Sure, friend," he said. "But we usually go looking for food together. It's just about time for dinner now. C'mon, before it gets dark."

Woot was relieved. "Wow, that's great," he said. "Thank you so much." He paused. He didn't want to be demanding, but he hoped the food was decent. "What do you expect to find? Safflower seeds, millet, maybe some maple peas?"

The feral pigeons exchanged glances.

"Uh, not exactly," Hipster said. "This ain't Wolfgang Puck. Let's go."

The feral pigeons led the way out an open window to the street as Woot followed behind.

They flew to an outside mall all the way downtown. In addition to some clothing stores and fast food joints, the mall contained a movie theater. The area outside the theater was the best bet for finding stray pieces of human food.

"Yo, look what I found," Hipster said. He picked up a piece of popcorn with his beak. Other pigeons mobbed him at the sight of it. He tried to defend his snack.

Woot was aghast. "Is this all you get to eat?" he asked. "Popcorn that the humans leave behind?"

"Sometimes we get rice," the dainty pigeon answered. "Uncooked. That's what the nice bird ladies feed us. But don't sweat it, handsome. We'll show you the ropes."

A manager from the movie theater came out the door with a broom and tried to scare the birds away. "Shoo, shoo. Get out of here, you nasty pigeons," he said. The flock dispersed, flying to the rooftops of neighboring buildings.

"This is what it's come down to for us," said Hipster. "We get no respect."

Woot, standing on the roof next to him replied, "Look, I appreciate you including me and all, but I've got to find my way back home. I got my friends and family there."

"Family?" asked the dainty pigeon. "Are you married?"

"Well, yes," said Woot.

The teenaged pigeon said, "Well, that's no problem. Most pigeons are paired up."

"Unfortunately, I'm still looking," the dainty pigeon said. "I was hoping to meet someone a bit better off than these guys."

Woot was very curious about this group of feral pigeons. All the pigeons he'd ever met were purebred and lived in lofts. He wondered what it was like to be free. He was eager to hear their stories. "How did you come to live in downtown Phoenix?" he asked. "Did you escape from a loft?"

The feral pigeons looked at each other and laughed.

"Escape from a loft? That's a good one," said Hipster. "No, we're what you call feral. Wild. Though some of us are wilder than others, hee-hee."

The teenager looked at Woot's feet. "What about you? Why do you have a green band around your ankle?"

"I'm a racing pigeon," Woot said. "The band is a sort of identification."

The teenager was impressed. "Wow, a racing pigeon," he said. "Specially bred. I've heard of you guys, but I never met one until now. I sure would look up to you."

Woot was humbled. "Well, don't," he said. "Obviously, I'm not that good – I got lost."

The dainty Pigeon touched him with her wing. "Don't be so hard on yourself," she said. "We all have bad days."

Woot smiled. Now he knew he was accepted. "You know, I never met any totally free pigeons before," he said. "How did you all meet each other?"

Hipster told his story. "I flew west from New York City. See, things were getting rough there in Washington Square Park. Some nice humans used to feed us, but then someone called the top brass in the city. Said they needed to crack down on our overpopulation problem. Called in some 'sterminators."

A hush fell over the birds. Their expressions turned grave.

Hipster continued. "That's right," he said. "They set traps. Tried to poison our food. I said to myself, "Go West, young bird" and eventually I landed here."

"It's not so bad," the dainty pigeon said. "We're a bit on the run more than I'd like, but we can usually find shelter and enough food to get by."

"Still, it ain't a cakewalk," Hipster admitted. "These cowboy-type humans don't use poison or traps, but they do like target shooting. And it ain't always clay pigeons that they use as targets."

The birds shuddered.

"They also mess with our sleeping arrangements," the teenaged pigeon said. He pointed with one wing to spikes and spires on the tops of buildings across the courtyard. "They put those up last year, thinking it would keep us out of this neighborhood. Why can't they just let us be?"

"No matter how many barriers they place, though," Hipster said, "we find somewhere to hole up for the night. They don't know whom they're dealing with."

He glanced in the direction of a shady-looking human who had entered the courtyard. The man carried a large fishing net in one hand. The movie theater manager approached the man. "Whatever you can catch, you're welcome to take," the manager said to the shady guy. "Just make it quick. I don't need an audience. Sometimes people get upset."

The shady guy looked around. "No problem. I'll be quick."

He reached inside his pocket and threw safflower seeds on the ground. The birds drooled, trying to resist the temptation.

"Did you see that?" asked the teenaged pigeon.

"I'm dying here," Hipster said.

"Safflower seeds," the dainty pigeon said. She sighed. "I can't remember how long it's been since I've indulged."

"I got a bad feeling about this guy," said Hipster. "Maybe the seeds are laced with poison."

Woot decided to step up to the plate. He wanted to help these nice birds who had welcomed him with acceptance. "Would you like me to scope it out?" he offered. "I can fly down there, taste one or two seeds, and if it seems safe you can follow."

"You'd do that for us?" asked Hipster. "What a boid! Go for it."

Woot flew to the ground to grab some seeds, but before he could fill his stomach, the shady guy threw the net over him. The other birds took off in fear.

"What a bummer," said the dainty pigeon as she retreated. "Sorry, handsome," she called back. "It was great meeting you."

After he caught Woot in his net, the shady guy shoved Woot into a burlap sack. He swung the sack over his shoulder and turned toward the movie theater manager. "Oh, well," the shady guy said. "At least I caught one of them. And it looked like the best of the bunch."

Chapter 8 – Pigeons with a Purpose

The shady guy pulled his van up to the back entrance of Tom's Country Feed Store with Woot in tow. Tom, the store owner, was tending to the livestock. All kinds of animals were for sale – no questions asked. As the shady guy approached, Tom greeted him. "What you got for me today?" he asked. He wiped his hands on his trousers.

"I only got one bird today, but he has an ankle band, so I think he's a purebred," the shady guy said. He handed Tom the burlap sack.

Tom peeked inside. "Yup. That's a racer, all right," he said. He handed the shady guy some money. Tom carried Woot to the pigeon section of the store. The pigeons were separated by type into three large cages. Each cage was six feet high. The first cage contained several breeds of fancy pigeon. A sign taped to the door read "fancy pigeons $25." The second cage contained banded birds, primarily blue-checked in color. A sign taped to this cage read "racing pigeons $30." The third cage contained feral pigeons, the kind found on the street. Some of the birds were covered in soot. Unlike the bins of water in the other two cages, water in this cage was murky, with a film of slime on the surface. The birds in this cage looked weak. Some even looked sick. The sign on this cage read "regular, plain pigeons $2."

A customer called for Tom. Distracted, Tom tossed Woot into the third cage by mistake. Instead of being in the second cage with the other racing pigeons, Woot was in the cage with the dirty pigeons. He looked around. "Hello, there, everyone," he said. "I'm Woot."

Some of the birds glanced at him with hopeless expressions on their little faces. Most were too weak to even acknowledge Woot's greeting.

"Can someone, anyone, please tell me what kind of place this is?" Woot asked.

A skinny gray pigeon responded. "Welcome to Tom's Country Feed Store, where no one's future is guaranteed."

"What's that supposed to mean?"

"It means you're trapped with us in the loser section. The only humans interested in us are those with bad intentions."

For the first time, Woot noticed the other two cages and understood that he was not with the other racers. "I don't mean to be rude," he said, "but I think I'm supposed to be in that cage next door."

The skinny bird laughed without mirth. "Isn't that poignant? Captivity the great equalizer. But you think you're in a special category, eh?"

Woot felt misunderstood. He wasn't "breedist." "I'm not saying I'm better than any of you. In fact, I just came from downtown Phoenix where I met your kind of ferals for the very first time. Very impressive bunch."

"Where do you think we came from?" the skinny bird asked. "Each of us here was living free up until we got caught. Granted, we were just getting by, but we did OK."

"Well, maybe some good people will buy you and put you in a nice loft," Woot suggested, trying to be helpful and hopeful.

"Ha! No way. This isn't my first rodeo, you know. I was here last month. A man bought me and a few of my friends. The purpose: dog training. But I escaped and was captured again!"

"Dog training? I don't understand."

"Did you just fall off the turnip truck?" the skinny bird asked. He sounded a little nasty, which might be understandable under his circumstances. "Humans use dogs to retrieve quail after they shoot them. They use our kind of pigeons to give the dogs practice before they go hunting together."

Woot was horrified. "Oh my God!" he cried. "We've got to get out of here."

"Good luck with that. We're not going anywhere tonight. Might as well make yourself comfortable."

Woot had no choice but to make the best of the tough situation. He jumped to an empty perch in the crowded space to settle in for the night.

The next morning, the store opened to a line of eager regular customers. Among them were a local hunter and his young daughter. Tom recognized them right away. He brought them over to the feral pigeon cage. Tom patted the hunter's shoulder. "Here you go," he said. Training pigeons for sale. Just two dollars apiece."

The hunter peered into the cage. "Sounds good," he said. "We'll take five. But try not to give us the sickest ones, OK? They need to have some fight left in them. I want to give the dogs a good practice session."

Tom walked into the cage. As sick as some of the birds were, they all made a frantic effort to stay out of Tom's grasp. Woot realized that the commotion provided a chance for escape. When Tom bent down to grab a few birds, Woot flew over Tom's head and out the door. The hunter's young daughter tried to block Woot's flight path. "Daddy," she cried out. "The pretty one is getting away!"

Woot looked back over his shoulder at the doomed feral pigeons. "I'm so sorry to leave you all behind," he said. "With all my heart, I wish you the best of luck."

He had no choice. There was nothing else he could do to help those poor birds. He beat his wings for maximum speed.

After about an hour of flying in what he hoped was the direction to Blythe, Woot came to a different section of the city. He looked down and saw an outdoor market that featured stands of exotic foods: produce, seafood, and poultry. In addition to live chickens, there were crates of live, plump, white king pigeons. King pigeons were a type of pigeon called "utility" pigeons, meaning they were bred specifically as food. Woot decided to investigate. He flew to the king pigeon area and peered inside a crate. A huge king pigeon looked back at him.

"Psst," the king pigeon whispered. "You, there. Can you get me out of here?"

Woot held his eye up to a gap in the crate. "Oh, hey there," he said. "What are you doing inside that crate?"

The king pigeon looked scared. "They're gonna sell me," he said.

"Sell you? What for? For training dogs? For racing?" Woot was beginning to learn all the uses of the different types of pigeons. "No offense, but you don't look trim enough to race."

"No, not to race, to eat."

Woot was confused. "You mean the humans want to eat you? I don't get it. You're not a chicken."

"Yeah, well tell that to them. Some humans like to eat us and the younger the better."

Still feeling bad from his encounter with Tom's Country Feed Store, Woot wanted to help this bird. "I'm willing to help. Do you have any ideas?"

"Well, maybe you can cause a distraction," the king pigeon suggested. "Just at the right time." He gulped. "When someone tries to…buy me."

Woot considered. "Uh, OK. I'll see what I can do."

He soon had his opportunity. A female human patron was exchanging money with the pigeon proprietor. The proprietor lifted the lid of the crate to let the woman select a pigeon. Just as she was about to do so, Woot hopped on top of her head and laid his tail feathers over her face. She screamed. The proprietor dropped the open crate and the king pigeon flew out.

"Thanks buddy," the king pigeon shouted on his way to freedom. "You're a lifesaver. Literally."

"Don't mention it," Woot called back. "And now I'm taking off too!"

Woot was getting a real education about what life could be like for pigeons that didn't live in a loft. True, life in a loft had lots of restrictions, but life for pigeons outside a loft seemed much tougher. He was an exceptionally smart bird, but this experience was taxing. He thought about his beautiful mate, Hilde. Was she worried about him? He'd never been away from her this long. And what about his best friend and human, Daniel? They'd always had an unspoken bond, but now that they could communicate, their friendship was even closer.

Woot was determined to get back. He tried to visualize a pathway to Blythe. He checked the position of the sun, adjusted his elevation, and surveyed the land below. Something didn't seem right. He must have made a wrong turn somewhere along the way. He squinted his eyes in concentration. Aha! He had made an error in his navigation plan when he left Tom's Country Feed Store. He course-corrected and changed direction once again.

Soon he passed over a suburban area. Down below, a human woman wore a long white dress, with a white veil attached to a crown on her head. A human male in a tuxedo stood next to her. The man reminded Woot of a tuxedo pigeon. Music was played by a group of humans sitting in a semicircle. An audience sat in white chairs behind the couple. Some of the chairs had balloons tied to the edges. Woot was fascinated. He couldn't recall ever seeing anything quite like this scene. He slowed down to stare. Pow! He collided with a cluster of pigeons. He couldn't believe it. Some of the birds were pure white and some were colored a pastel pink.

A white, tough broad of a wedding release homing pigeon addressed him first. "Hey, buddy, look where you're going!" she demanded.

Woot was a little taken aback. "Excuse me, ma'am, but I believe it is you who crashed into me," he said politely.

Penny – a pretty, petite, white wedding release homer – tried to diffuse the tension. "Don't mind her," she said to Woot. "We're just doing our jobs. Any mishaps spoil the show. I'm Penny, by the way."

"I'm Woot. You're homing pigeons, right? Like me."

Penny nodded.

"Wow," said Woot, "you're all so classy."

The tough broad was appeased. "Thanks," she said. "Didn't mean to be rude. Just focused on our job."

"So, you're not racing?" Woot asked.

"Oh, heavens, no," Penny answered. "That's kind of low class, don't you think? We're specially trained to delight audiences at weddings, funerals, and bar mitzvahs."

Woot's eyes widened. "You don't say. Do you live in a loft?"

"We sure do," said Penny. "And it's pretty nice. It has all the amenities. Jacuzzi, air-conditioning in the summer, heat in the winter."

A large, pastel-pink male pigeon piped up. "Only problem is some of us are dyed pink, and it's a tough color to wear."

"Look, everyone's gotta earn a living somehow," the tough-broad homing pigeon said.

"Yeah, and boy did we earn ours," the pink male pigeon said. "We just put on a real great show for the humans."

"Well, it's been nice talking to you," Penny said, "but we should really get back before dark."

Woot was not eager to see them leave. All pigeons prefer being part of a flock, and he was no exception. Besides, he was lonely. Since these were homing pigeons, too, it would be good to get their opinion about his flight plan. "Hey, before you go, do you think you can confirm my directions to Blythe, California?" he asked.

"Blythe?" the tough broad repeated. "Never heard of it."

Woot realized that it was getting late. He'd need a place to roost for the night. "Well, how about I come back with you, just for the night?" he asked. "I sure could use a good meal and a good night's sleep in a comfortable loft." He had an idea. "Say, I could even be in your shows to pay my way."

The wedding release birds looked Woot up and down. There was a moment of uncomfortable silence. Finally, the tough-broad homer spoke up. "Um, I don't think that's going to work," she said. "I'm sure you're very fast and all, but you don't have the right look."

Woot opened his eyes wide. "You mean because I'm...blue-checked?"

"Don't feel bad about it," the macho bird said. "At least you'll never be dyed pink."

With that, the birds flew off.

.

Chapter 9 – Linda's Wise Words

Daniel and Jed sat in the kitchen eating dinner. The setting sun shot rays of orange light through the window. Despite the room's warm glow, the mood was somber. Daniel picked at his food.

"What's the matter, son?" Jed began. "No appetite? That's not like you. Come to think of it, you been acting strange ever since the weekend."

Daniel murmured under his breath. "Nothing's the matter."

"Now come on," Jed persisted. "Don't tell me nothing. I can tell something's bugging you."

Daniel didn't answer.

Jed took a swig of beer. "Is it because we didn't win the race?" He shoveled some ground beef into his mouth and chewed as he spoke. "Don't know why you're so grumpy about that. I'm the one who was counting on that money."

Daniel looked at his father. Part of him wanted to tell his father the truth. But could he risk his father's scorn? "It's not about money," he said. "You're not going to understand. You'll just think I'm weird like some of the kids at school do."

Jed narrowed his eyes. "You're upset about the missing bird?" he challenged. "The blue-checked homer. The one you call Woot."

Daniel didn't deny it.

"Aw, jeez," Jed continued. "I warned you about this more than once. You can't get attached to any one bird. They ain't that important."

How could Woot not be important? Daniel was mad enough to stand up to his father. "He was important to me," Daniel insisted. "I don't get why you can't see that."

"You need to spend more time with kids your own age."

"Are you saying you don't want to spend time with me?"

"I'm not saying that at all," Jed said. "You're taking it the wrong way. I thought we had this pigeon hobby in common, but we're not on the same page at all."

"I enjoy taking care of them, watching how they act. Woot was my pet, almost like a friend," Daniel tried to explain.

"That just sounds lame to *me,*" Jed replied. "You used to look up to me and listen to what I say. Now it's like you think the birds have feelings or something. Maybe it *is* weird."

Daniel sucked in his breath. He picked up his dinner plate and pushed his chair back with his hip. He put his plate in the dishwasher and wordlessly left the room.

Jed called after him. "Daniel! Don't be like that. Come back and discuss this like a man!"

A few hours later, Daniel sat on his bed with his arms crossed and a frown on his face. If his father was this judgmental about treating the birds like pets, what would he say if he knew Daniel could communicate with animals?

As crazy as it initially seemed, Daniel had gotten used to his new ability. If he didn't think too much about it, he was okay. Whenever he did, though, he would feel a shiver run down his spine. Daniel had heard about paranormal phenomena...things like ESP and people using their minds to move objects. Maybe he had a form of ESP. Could it be that his vivid imagination and sensitivity toward animals was just much stronger than usual?

He longed to confide in someone, but he knew it was too risky. Would Mr. Price understand and even be able to provide an explanation? How about Elena? No. Best to keep his secret to himself, and to the birds. He looked at the clock on the dresser across the room. Jed must be asleep by now. Daniel got up and headed to the loft. He wanted to check in on the pigeons – especially Woot's mate, Hilde – to see how they were feeling about Woot's absence.

"I'm so worried," Hilde said. "I just can't sleep. Where is he? Is he safe? What if he's hurt? Or worse –"

Daniel stroked her feathers to reassure her. "I'm worried too. But I know he's smart, he's strong, and he's fast."

"Then why isn't he back?" Hilde persisted.

Daniel didn't know what to say.

Even Spirit was upset. "I know I gave him a hard time," he said. "But I miss him too."

Sally said, "Look, y'all. He has numbers on his ankle band. If something happened to him, someone would track down Daniel's father."

Daniel thought about Sally's logic. She gave him an idea. "That's a good point," he said. "I can put a lost pigeon ad on Craigslist or on some of those websites for pigeon fanciers."

"That's right," Spirit added. "It's only been a few days. Maybe he went on an adventure. Maybe he's bringing back new nesting material or something."

Hilde looked a little reassured, but not entirely so. Daniel gave her a gentle pat on her head before he placed her back on her perch.

The following day, Jed worked in his backyard repairing his patio. While he was busy mixing cement, Linda came up the driveway in her pickup truck.

"Hey, Linda," said Jed, wiping his hands with a cloth. "This is a pleasant surprise."

"Hi, Jed," Linda greeted him back. "Hope you don't mind me popping by like this unannounced, but I was in your neck of the woods."

"Glad to see you," Jed replied.

"Say," she began, "I heard your star homer got lost after the Southwest Regional Race."

"Yeah, that's true. Pretty big disappointment."

"How's Daniel taking it?"

"Not so great. He had a real shining for that bird."

Linda nodded. "I can relate to how he feels. When my dog Paulo got lost I cried for a week."

"Yeah, but it ain't the same thing. You can't compare a pigeon to a dog."

"I don't know. Sometimes I see real intelligence in the birds' eyes."

Jed looked skeptical.

"Come here – I'll show you." Linda led Jed over to the loft. She stepped inside. "Do you mind?" she asked. Jed shook his head. She picked Spirit up and lifted him to Jed's face. "Take this one, for example," she said. "Look at his face."

Spirit tipped his head in her direction as if listening to the conversation. Linda stroked the top of his head with an index finger. Spirit closed his eyes in pleasure.

"I'm tempted to swap you that bird since you like him so much," Jed said. "But I can't risk Daniel getting upset about another bird."

"Pardon my saying this, Jed, but do you think you're being a little hard on him?"

Jed pursed his lips. "Patrice would have said the same thing. But since she's gone and it's just me and him, I see it as my job to make him strong."

"Maybe I'm missing something," Linda said. "I never did fully grasp the male brain, but I don't see kindness and compassion as weak."

Jed sighed. "I'm not as bad as some of those others, Linda. Personally, I don't cull. Well, rarely."

"Do you even have your personal favorites, at all?"

"No. That's not how my father passed the sport down. It's about winning."

"It's a little different for me," Linda said. "After my kids grew up and left home I needed something to take care of. Shoot, what was I going to do, take up gardening? I don't have a green thumb. Pigeon-keeping became my hobby."

"OK, so it's a hobby for you too."

"Yes, but I enjoy the nurturing part. And when I look at my favorites, I see lights on and somebody home."

"I really like you, Linda, I do. But that sounds a little nuts."

"OK, you're entitled to your opinion. But do me a favor. Go a little easier on that great kid of yours. They're up and out of the house before you know it."

"Yep. In fact, don't say anything to anyone, but at the next association meeting I'm gonna surprise him with a new purebred blue-checked squab," Jed said.

"I'll be darned. Maybe there's a sensitive guy buried somewhere deep within you, Jed."

Jed laughed. "Don't get too carried away. I still don't think a pigeon should be treated like a dog."

Linda rolled her eyes and headed back to her truck.

Chapter 10 – Woot In Suburbia

After the wedding release pigeons left him, Woot continued his journey home. He measured the position of the sun and tried to confirm a pathway west. His stomach growled. His beak was parched. He needed to eat and drink something soon. He checked to make sure that there were no predators around. There weren't any, so he zoomed down to a suburban neighborhood to search for food. One house looked especially promising. It was an adobe ranch house that had a bird feeder hanging from a tree in the backyard. The bird feeder was easy to spot, because a noisy flock of quails – and an unruly flock of doves – was gathered below it on the ground. They pecked at the fallen seed. Woot would later learn that the house belonged to Susan and Ralph Freeman, a childless couple who thought of their pets and rescued animals as family members.

Woot eagerly joined the crowd. Doves and quail were close relatives of pigeons. He had heard somewhere that they even ate the same food. "Mind if I join you?" he asked the flocks. "I'm starving."

Cackling quail sounds morphed into English. A female quail and her mate smiled at Woot. "No problem," the female quail replied. "There's plenty here."

"What a great setup!" Woot said.

"Yes," said the male quail. "It's like this every day. Like clockwork, the lady of the house fills this bucket thing and *voilà*, we've got our *dejéuner*. That's 'lunch' in French, you know."

A large mourning dove bopped over to Woot. He pointed with his beak to a window of the house, where a woman was looking out. "See that lady over there?" he asked. "She's the one who feeds us. And we have plenty to drink too."

Almost as though to prove the point, the doves headed over to the backyard swimming pool and dipped into the shallow area. They splashed happily. Woot joined them and took a long drink from the pool.

He was relieved to take a break, but the sun was beginning to set. The warm glow of dusk cast a yellow light on the patio furniture. The quail and doves separated into two groups.

"Time to go," said the male quail. "We've got to get situated for the night."

In military formation, the quail marched away. They cackled loudly as they left.

The large mourning dove said, "Us too. Let's go find a place to roost."

The doves flew away in a flash, making a sound like chimes as their wings fluttered in unison.

Woot was left standing alone on the patio pavement. He wished that there were other pigeons around. He had no flock. He rotated his head in different directions as he searched for a place to perch for the night. "Well, I'll be darned," he thought to himself. "Here I am again on my own. Wasn't there a song like that?"

He saw a gap in the roof. A missing tile created a space that could serve as his roosting spot. He flew there in a flash. But his attempt to cheer himself up didn't work. He fought off tears. Not only did he miss Hilde and the other pigeons in the loft, but he also really missed Daniel.

The next morning at the Freemans' house, Mrs. Freeman peered outside the window for the sheer pleasure of viewing any wildlife that might come by. Susan Freeman was a kind, middle-aged woman who was just a little bit odd. While it wasn't terribly unusual to appreciate wildlife, Susan Freeman had a habit of going to extremes. She sometimes brought more animals indoors than she and her husband could handle. On this sunny day, she was enjoying the ground flock of mourning doves as they gobbled up fallen seeds. Then she spotted Woot. She was perplexed. They didn't ever see pigeons in this suburb. Pigeons tended to flock to the city, where there weren't as many predators.

She called to her husband, Ralph. "Honey, come here for a minute. There's a huge pigeon mixed in with the mourning doves."

Her husband, a fat and kindly middle-aged man, was in the other room watching Netflix. Not really paying attention to his wife, he uttered, "Mm-hmm."

"It's odd," she continued. "You know we don't have pigeons up here in the hills. And he doesn't look like a regular pigeon. Come here – take a look. He's larger and his feathers are glossier."

She opened the sliding door to her backyard and stuck her head out for a few seconds to get a better look. Not wanting to scare the birds away, she stepped back inside. "He's got a green band around his ankle! What could that mean? Do you think he's part of a research project?"

"Mm-hmm. Could be," Mr. Freeman said from the other room.

"Ralph!" she called with urgency. "Please come here. This is important to me."

Mr. Freeman sighed and joined his wife in the kitchen. He peered outside the glass door. "We should probably catch it," he said. "If it's part of a research study, someone could be missing it." He opened the sliding door and rushed outside. He ran toward the bird and extended his arms as if to gather him up. "Come here!" he called to Woot. "It's OK!"

Most of the quail and doves frantically flew away. Some of the quail ran around in confused circles on the ground.

Woot looked in Mr. Freeman's direction. He was interested in meeting him. He'd had positive experiences with humans before, especially Daniel, but he was put off by Mr. Freeman's high energy. He flew up a tree. Once there, he spoke to some quail and doves perched on the branches. "Who's that human guy?"

A female quail answered him. "That's the lady's mate."

"Since they're feeding you, should we assume he's friendly?" Woot asked.

"Maybe," said a male quail, "but I don't take chances like that. You know how humans are. They're so unpredictable."

Woot had to admit that the quail had a point. He flew back to his roof spot to hide.

Later that day Mrs. Freeman filled the feeder with more seed. She went back inside and watched from the glass sliding door. Some small birds, sparrows and finches, pecked at the feeder. They spilled some of the seeds onto the ground. Woot and the flock of mourning doves had reconvened there for an evening feast. Mrs. Freeman noticed them. She walked very slowly and placed their own small dish of seeds on the patio. She backed up and slipped inside to observe from the window.

Woot spoke to the mourning doves as he ate. "There's that lady again."

"Relax. She's harmless. In fact, she's a bird lover," one of the doves said.

"Oh yeah?" Woot considered. "Maybe she can help me get back home."

"I don't know if I'd go that far," the dove said. He finished eating and flew off. The other doves followed, leaving Woot to himself.

Woot approached the pool to take a drink. He splashed around the shallow area. It was a great place for a bath. Mrs. Freeman was still watching. "Ralph! Ralph! Come quick. There's that pigeon again."

Mr. Freeman ran into the kitchen and looked out the window alongside his wife. "So it is," he said. "OK, let's corner him. You slip out the garage door and chase him in my direction. I'll be ready with the pool net."

Woot was oblivious to their plan. He munched happily on the seeds in his dish. Mrs. Freeman slowly crept toward him. She looked him straight in the eye. He saw her and hopped in the other direction toward Mr. Freeman. Before Woot could fly away, Mr. Freeman caught him with the net.

"Don't worry, little bird," Ralph Freeman said softly to Woot. "We won't hurt you." Gingerly, he held Woot and tried to read the numbers on his ankle band. "Susan, grab a pen," he called out. "I'll read you the numbers." He read off the numbers to his wife.

"I've got it," Mrs. Freeman said. "I'll search the Internet and try to see what it means." She went inside.

Mr. Freeman placed Woot in a large dog crate. He rested the crate on their patio table and joined his wife inside. After a couple of hours of research, the Freemans learned about the sport of pigeon racing.

"Can you imagine there's such a thing as pigeon racing?" Mrs. Freeman asked her husband. "Who would have guessed?"

They huddled together in front of a computer screen.

"Unbelievable," said Mr. Freeman. "It says here, based on the numbers, that this bird was part of a club in southeastern California. That's over a hundred and fifty miles from here."

"We can call the club and they'll determine whose bird this is," Mrs. Freeman said.

She reached for her cell phone and dialed the Southeastern California Pigeon Association.

Nando answered. "Hello. Yes, I'm the head of the club. Yeah…some of us have racing pigeons. Hold on. OK, you want to read me those numbers? Wait. Just let me grab my ledger." He reached for a notebook and returned to the phone call. "OK, I'm ready. Go ahead and read me the numbers." Nando looked at the ledger as he listened. "Got it. That's Jed Wilson's bird. I'll give him a call for you, so he can come pick it up. OK. You're welcome, and thank you for calling."

Nando hung up and dialed Jed. "Jed? Check this out. A lady all the way in the burbs of Phoenix has one of your birds from last week's race. She wants to know if you want it back."

Jed replied, "You know the deal, Nando. The bird's a loser. Why would I want it back?"

Jed didn't notice Daniel in the doorway, eavesdropping.

"I don't know what you should tell her," Jed said. "Tell her anything you want."

"Dad! What are you doing?" Daniel exclaimed. "That could be Woot. We've got to go get him!"

Jed spoke to Nando on the phone. "I've got to go. I'll call you back."

He hung up and turned to face Daniel. "I don't know how many times we've got to go through this. That bird had a job to do and that job was to win races. He couldn't even find his way back home at all, let alone win the race. So, you tell me. What kind of a homing pigeon is he?"

"He's still my bird and he belongs here at our loft. Why can't we go get him?"

"That lady lives over a hundred miles away in Phoenix. There's no way I'm driving all the way out there for a failed homing pigeon. Sorry. End of conversation."

Daniel stormed off.

Back at the Freeman's it was house-cleaning day. Mrs. Freeman opened the door to a large guest suite at the far end of her home. There were all kinds of rescued and rehabilitated animals living in the suite. It wasn't a hoarding situation, but it was crowded. Mrs. Freeman sneezed and wiped her eyes. Truth be told, although she didn't like to admit it, she was allergic to some of the animals. She never let that stop her rescue efforts though.

A dog and a couple of cats roamed the floor. One large cage, protected by hardware cloth, contained two ferrets. A baby javelina recuperated from an injury in an incubator. Javelinas, or peccaries, resemble pigs but are not actually related to them. They are part of a completely different class of animal that is found in South America and in parts of the American Southwest.

The suite also housed several birdcages stacked on shelves, out of reach of the cats. The birds included an African grey parrot, a couple of love birds, and some budgies. Mr. and Mrs. Freeman had placed Woot in a huge, top-grade bird cage in the bird section.

"Well, I guess they didn't want the bird back," Mrs. Freeman said to her husband.

"That's OK," Mr. Freeman replied. "He'll have a nice home here with us. From what I've read, it sounds like these birds do nicely inside as pets. Apparently, they can even be trained to wear pigeon pants and get time out of the cage."

Woot thought to himself, "Pants? No way. I'm the type who goes *au naturel*."

"Maybe we can train him to do tricks," Mr. Freeman suggested. "I don't think they talk, though, like parrots."

Mrs. Freeman leaned toward Woot. She spoke to him in a baby voice. "Look at your new, beautiful home, you sweet bird."

Woot shouted out loud. "No, no! It's just a big cage. Please let me out of here."

"Listen, Susan," Mr. Freeman said. "He's cooing. It's almost as though he knows what a great home we're going to give him."

Woot just sighed to himself.

Chapter 11 – Daniel's Search for Woot

Daniel hadn't discussed Woot's absence with anyone but his father. He knew that the kids at school wouldn't understand. But one afternoon Elena approached him as he was collecting books from his locker. They spoke to each other in the hallway.

"So, how did Woot do in the big race?" Elena asked in an excited voice.

"Not so great," Daniel admitted. He looked down at the ground. He wondered if he could confide in her. He decided to take a chance. "But that doesn't even matter to me. He hasn't come back yet!"

Elena gasped. "Oh no! Has that ever happened before?"

"No, but this was his first real race," Daniel explained. "He's always come back after we let him out, and he came back after the training exercise, too."

"I'm so sorry! But don't worry. I'm sure he'll find his way back to you."

"I'm not so sure," Daniel said. "And even if he does, I'm not sure my dad will let me keep him."

Elena's mouth opened in inquiry just as Frankie approached. "Well, if it isn't the best-looking girl in school talking to the biggest loser," he taunted. "You're both pathetic."

Despite Frankie's larger size, Daniel didn't retreat. He just stayed silent.

"So that's it?" Frankie persisted. "You're not even going to say anything?"

"There's no point in fighting with you," Daniel said. "I have bigger problems than you."

Frankie slammed Daniel's open locker door shut. "Still not going to do anything?" he demanded.

Elena stomped her foot. "What's wrong with you?" she asked Frankie. "What happened to you to make you so evil?"

"I'm not evil. I'm just tough when I got problems. Unlike this dude." Frankie pointed his chin at Daniel. "You think you have problems? Aw, your little birdie flew away. You have no idea what real problems are."

Daniel and Elena exchanged subtle surprised glances at this hint of a troubled home life.

"Look," Daniel began, "I'm sorry to hear you have problems. For me, my birds make me feel better about things." He looked away for a moment. "I mean, you can even come by my house to check them out."

Frankie raised his eyebrows. "You're really inviting me over...even after I been so rotten to you?"

Daniel shrugged, not knowing what to else say. Frankie just shook his head and walked away.

Later that evening, Daniel sat on his bed with his head resting on his hands. What would life be like without Woot, especially now that they'd been able to understand each other? It was even more frustrating because he knew approximately where Woot was located. He had to act now. Even if it meant handling things on his own, he would bring Woot home. If his father wouldn't drive him to Phoenix, he'd have to get there himself. Somehow. He thought about it and an idea jumped into his head. What was to stop him from hiking to the highway and then hitching a ride to Phoenix?

Daniel pulled camping supplies out of his closet and dresser drawers. He had everything he needed: backpack, tent, canteen. Softly, he moved down the stairs to the kitchen. He filled his canteen with water and packed his backpack with trail mix and prepackaged camping food. He hoisted the backpack onto his shoulders. He grabbed his cell phone and checked the GPS app. Quietly, so he wouldn't awaken Jed, Daniel slipped out the front door and headed to the loft.

Once inside the loft, he bid goodbye to the pigeons. "Guys, I'm heading out to look for Woot. I wanted you to know he's not been abandoned."

Spirit was concerned. "Daniel, are you sure it's safe out there by yourself? What if you get lost also?"

"Don't worry, I'm a very experienced hiker. I need some time alone, anyway, to think things through."

The birds still looked worried. Daniel tried to reassure them. "I'm sure I can get myself to this family in Phoenix that's keeping him."

"But, Daniel, none of us should be away from the flock for too long," Hilde said. "I'm worried about Woot, but now I'll be worried about you too."

"I've been camping since before I could talk. Believe me, if I could drive I would, but that's not possible."

"You sure you know how to get there?" asked Spirit.

"I overheard Nando tell Dad what neighborhood that lady lives in. I figure I'll need to camp out in the desert for a couple of nights, but then I'll be able to hitch a ride to Phoenix once I get to the highway."

"Please be careful," Hilde pleaded.

"I will. Don't forget our special rhyme – Daniel said.

"You mean 'Distance near or far, we can create / a pathway home to our lofty gates?'" Spirit asked.

"Yes," Daniel said. "Life's all about planning. I have everything I need for this trip, including a pathway home." He nodded his head in determination and closed the door to the loft.

Daniel and Jed lived in a rural area on the outskirts of Blythe, California. Their house was located far from any main roads, let alone the highway. Daniel estimated that it would take two days to hike through the desert before he would reach the interstate. While hitchhiking is generally a risky endeavor, it was a common practice in Daniel's neighborhood. Not too many strangers came their way.

Daniel set off with long, confident strides to search for Woot. He meant it when he told the pigeons that he'd been camping for many years. He had to admit, though, this

156

was the longest trip he'd ever made. He found the trail that headed south toward I-10, the main highway connecting Blythe to Phoenix. He hiked long and hard, using the flashlight app on his iPhone and the moonlight to guide his path.

After about three hours or so, he was tired. He decided to rest under an ocotillo tree and he turned off his cell phone to save the battery. He looked up at the sky and took in the glittering stars. He took a few good, long swigs from his canteen. It felt so good to take a break, but he was keen to cover as much distance as possible. The sooner he got there, the better. Snakes and other critters came out at night. Also, he wanted to get to the Freemans' house before they made other choices about Woot's future. He got up after a few minutes and hiked on.

Soon his shoulders slumped with fatigue. He set his backpack on the ground and stretched his arms. He surveyed the desert landscape. This hike was more challenging than he had expected. After catching a few breaths, he hoisted his backpack and adjusted the shoulder straps. Just as his attention was focused on his pack, a large rattlesnake slithered over and spoke to him. "Psst. You there. What are you doing out here in the boonies all by yourself?"

Daniel jumped back. "Whoa! Uh, I'm headed toward Phoenix. Do you know where that is?"

"Nope. I'm a country snake, myself. I try to stay away from the big city. Too dangerous."

"Uh, yeah. Good point. Well, nice meeting you," Daniel said as he moved away. That wasn't quite true, but it was the polite thing to say. He didn't need to make enemies with a rattlesnake.

"A word of advice," the rattlesnake said. "You might want to find a place to settle in for the night. No telling what you could step on out here in the desert. There are spiders and scorpions all over, you know."

Daniel didn't appreciate the snake's attempt at irony. "Really? Spiders and scorpions? You don't say. Well, they don't bother me as much as snakes do."

Daniel trekked on. He was exhausted, and he knew the snake was right. He needed to find a place to camp for the night. He hiked another half-mile or so and came across a small cave. Daniel propped his iPhone up between two rocks, so he could continue to use it as a flashlight. He unpacked his sleeping bag. As he bent down to peek into the mouth of the cave, he caught a whiff of something nasty. The cave was inhabited by a family of javelinas, those piglike animals famous for their poor vision and excellent sense of smell. And their pungent, smelly bodies. They were also infamous for their territoriality, especially when they had young ones to defend. Daniel tended to like them, though, as he was a fan of most animals.

A large, male javelina popped his head out of the cave. "Uh, excuse me, this cave's taken," he said.

A female popped up next to him. "Yeah, unless you have a reservation?"

A troop of little javelinas peered out at Daniel from inside the cave. They giggled at their mother's joke. Daniel sniffed the air. "I was just looking for a place to sleep for the night," he said.

The javelina troop emerged from the cave and encircled Daniel.

"You need to move it along, buddy," the male javelina said. "I've got a family to protect here, and if past history is any predictor of future behavior, I don't trust you around them."

"Isn't there any way we can share this cave?" Daniel asked. "It makes for such a great shelter."

The female javelina bared her teeth. "I don't think so. Why should we share with you? It's not like your kind have been nice to us."

"That's right," the large male said. "Technically, we're not related to pigs. But that hasn't stopped people from seeing bacon when they look at us."

"I'm not like that, though," Daniel pointed out. "I don't mean you any harm."

"Oh no?" the female replied. "You a vegetarian?"

"Well, no –"

"Just as I thought," she said. "Tonight, you see us as friends. As soon as you get hungry enough, you'll see us as lunch. Like I said, move it along."

"No problem. I was just leaving." Daniel pulled his backpack up onto his shoulders and went on his way. He'd have to find another place to lay down his sleeping bag and his weary bones. He hiked another quarter of a mile and came across a cottonwood tree. It wasn't as good as a cave, but it offered some shelter. He looked up at the sky. It didn't seem like rain or a storm would be coming. This would have to do. He was done for the night. He spread out his sleeping bag and tucked himself inside. He slept soundly.

The next morning, the scorching sun roused Daniel from his deep slumber. He yawned and stretched his arms. He was still exhausted, even after a full night's sleep. His muscles ached. Maybe he wasn't in as good shape as he thought he was. He helped himself to a long swig of water from his canteen. He munched on some trail mix, and then glanced at his watch. He'd better pick up the pace. He was running through his supplies faster than he'd expected to. He consulted the GPS app on his cell phone. It directed him southeast, with ten more miles to go until the highway.

Daniel packed up his gear and started hiking. There were a couple of forks in the trail system that he wasn't too sure about. He made the best decisions he could and then focused on his chosen path. After a long but uneventful day of trekking through the desert, the sun began to set. Daniel searched for a new place to camp. He spotted some rock formations in the near distance that he thought would make for a good shelter. As he approached the boulders, he saw two ring-necked doves perched on an adjacent bush. Doves were closely related to pigeons, and Daniel was glad to see the familiar birds. He was hopeful they'd be friendly.

"Hey, you there – you doves," he said.

"Why, hello," the smaller one said.

"Can you tell me if I'm on the right track to I-10 East?" Daniel asked. "I'm heading toward Phoenix."

"Phoenix? That's miles and miles away from here."

"Yeah, I know. Never mind. Is it OK with you if I camp out here for the night?"

"Doesn't bother us," the dove replied.

Daniel climbed the boulders, looking for a flat surface. One of the straps of his backpack was digging into his shoulder. He turned his neck, trying to adjust it. The move tipped him off balance. He skidded on the rocks, jamming his leg in a crevice of a boulder. His backpack tumbled down the hill, several feet out of reach. He screamed out in pain. "Help!!"

Daniel shivered in the desert cold. He twisted right, then left, trying to find a position that wasn't too uncomfortable. The lower part of his leg throbbed with pain. He tried not to panic. He'd read somewhere once that panic only made matters worse. Better to keep a cool head. Bile formed in his throat. He hoped he wouldn't throw up. He closed his eyes and thought of Woot. What was that funny rap about the virtue of pigeons? The rap was a little silly, but it made Daniel feel better, especially that part about navigation. "Distance near or far, we can create / a pathway home to our lofty gates."

Chapter 12 – Jed's Search for Daniel

Back at the Wilson home, it didn't take long for Jed to realize that Daniel was missing. Jed became frantic and started searching everywhere. First, he popped his head into the loft to make sure Daniel wasn't inside with the pigeons. "Daniel! Daniel! Where are you?" he called. Seeing that Daniel wasn't there, Jed rushed inside the house. He bounded the stairs two at a time to Daniel's bedroom. He ran into the room and saw the unmade bed. He threw open the closet door and rummaged through Daniel's stuff. Jed realized that Daniel's camping gear was missing. "Oh, no. What has he done?" he screamed silently inside his head.

Jed didn't know exactly where to turn for help. He knew Daniel was friends with that girl, Elena, but he did not have her phone number. Come to think of it, he didn't have the phone numbers of any of Daniel's acquaintances. He'd never needed to before. Jed decided to go to Daniel's school to see whether any of the kids knew where he might have gone. He called the school to let them know he was on his way.

Jed made his way to Daniel's homeroom class. Mr. Price gave the introduction. "Folks, I'd like to introduce you to Jed Wilson. He's Daniel's father."

Jed was a little nervous. He wasn't used to being around so many kids. He cleared his throat. "Um, yup. See, Daniel went camping by himself a couple of days ago. It's not like him to be gone this long, so I wondered if he said anything to any of you about where he was going."

Several of the students looked concerned. Elena's face fell.

"Elena, did he say anything to you?" Mr. Price asked, noticing her expression.

Before she could answer, Henry interrupted. He said, snidely, under his breath, "I bet he was looking for more pigeons."

Both Elena and Mr. Price shot him dirty looks. Jed just looked confused.

"He didn't say anything to me, Mr. Wilson," Elena said finally. "Was he upset or something?"

Jed was growing frustrated. The kids were his last hope. But they didn't seem to know anything. Jed looked around the room. "The only thing I can think of," he said, "is he was upset about this bird that didn't make it back from the race. He and I don't see eye to eye about that and, truth be told, it kind of pisses me off."

Something about Jed's tone and choice of words alarmed Frankie. He wasn't a big Daniel fan, but he liked adult male authority and aggressiveness even less. Suddenly, Jed became the target for Frankie's anger, instead of Daniel. "Why you pissed off, man?" Frankie demanded. "It's his bird. Why can't he miss it?"

Jed looked in Frankie's direction, trying to see who had the audacity to talk to him with that tone of voice. "Who said that?" he yelled. He moved with swift strong strides toward the back of the class, where Frankie was sitting. "Whoever said that should be prepared to take it outside."

"Now Mr. Wilson, "Mr. Price interjected. "I know you're upset, but please remember that this is a school. We seek rational solutions to our problems."

Jed just frowned. "You kids are no help at all. What a waste of my time." He stormed out of the classroom.

Frankie looked at Elena. "Wow. Daniel's father is kind of a jerk," he said to her.

Meanwhile, at the Freemans' house in suburbia, Woot was stuck in his cage in the guest suite with all the other animals. He had mixed feelings. After meeting so many less fortunate pigeons during his travels, he knew it could be worse. After all, he had plenty of food, water, and company. But he was very lonely for home. He missed his mate and friends, especially Daniel. Woot felt trapped.

The Freemans' dog sat near him on a couch.

"Hey you – dog," Woot said. "Do you think you can help me?"

The dog drooled and smiled. "Sure 'nuff. Wassup?"

"Can you chew through this wire so I can get out of here?" Woot asked.

"Why would you want to leave?" the dog asked. "You've got it made here. This family is good people. They'll take good care of you."

"Yeah, I know. It's nice here, but I've got a whole life back in Blythe. I've got a mate and a best friend, who also just happens to be a human."

"Gee, I don't know," the dog said. "I'm pretty good at chewing things, but my specialty is furniture. Any kind. Couches, chairs, even beds. I never chewed through a cage before."

"Well, do you think you could give it a try?" Woot asked.

"I dunno. I might get in trouble with the missus."

"Oh, come on," Woot persisted. "Take your chewing ability to the next level. If you free me, I'll fly to the top of the microwave and bring you back a doggie treat. Isn't that where they hide your treats?"

That convinced the dog. "Sure, why not? There's always a first time." The dog chewed a small hole in the cage. He picked at his teeth. "Hmm. Not bad. It's kind of like an industrial-grade dental floss," he noted. The dog tried to enlarge the hole even more.

Success! Woot escaped from the cage. He flew to the top of the microwave and pulled a dog chew out of a bag with his beak. He dropped the treat in front of the dog. "See ya!" Woot shouted. He squeezed out of a slightly open window that lent a bit of fresh air to the room. He was free again.

Later that evening, Jed, Nando, and Clint gathered on Jed's patio outside the loft. Jed wanted his friends' help in finding Daniel. He had also called the police. Three police officers came up to the house. The plan was to combine forces and conduct a search. Armed with flashlights, cell phones, and canteens, they prepared to disperse.

Before they set off, Chief of Police Bloom questioned Jed. "You say the last time you saw your boy was three days ago?"

"Yep," Jed answered.

"Has he run away from home before?" Chief Bloom asked.

Jed put his hand on his forehead and shook his head. "He's gone camping alone before, longer than that, but it's not like him to just take off without telling me."

"Was he upset about something? It would be helpful to understand his state of mind so we have something to go on."

Jed sighed. "He was upset about one of our racing pigeons. It was his favorite bird and it didn't return after the Southwest Regional race."

"The bird was *racing*?" Chief Bloom looked confused. "Never mind. Doesn't matter. We'll do our best to find him."

The police, Jed, and his friends set off. Therefore, there were no humans around when Woot returned to the loft and swooped into the flight cage. He landed squarely on the floor and looked around the loft. The birds were ecstatic. Spirit and Sally threw hay and straw in the air like confetti. The cooing was deafening. The birds clapped their wings in applause. Woot and Hilde touched beaks.

"Woot! My darling! I was so worried about you," Hilde cried.

"I'm fine." Woot replied. "I got caught in a dust storm. Really knocked me down. I had quite an adventure. You wouldn't believe the kinds of pigeons I met."

Spirit high-fived Woot with his wing, then broke the news about Daniel. "Now you're back, but Daniel's missing. We think he went looking for you! He was devastated when you didn't return from the race."

"What?" Woot asked, with a confused look on his face.

"We were all so worried about you," Hilde said. "Of course, deep down I knew you'd be back. Daniel took it harder."

"Well, I've got to find him!" Woot exclaimed. "Do you have any idea which direction he went?"

"I think he went southeast, toward Phoenix," Spirit said. "At least that's how it looked to me."

"You can't do anything tonight, Woot," Hilde said. "You know we don't see well in the dark. Why not eat and drink something and head out in the morning?"

"I hate having to do that," Woot said, "but I guess I don't have much of a choice."

As the pigeons plotted their strategy to find Daniel, Jed drove his truck down a desert dirt road to look for his son. From time to time he would pull over, jump out, and search the terrain with his flashlight. He performed this action three or four times. On his last stop, he saw nothing but barren hillside. Discouraged, he jumped back into his truck and drove away. A cloud of dust trailed behind.

About a mile away, Chief Bloom stood with his officers outside his vehicle. "You think the father checks out?" he asked. "You know the statistics on these missing-kids cases –"

"He doesn't have any priors," Officer Davis replied. "But I admit there's something strange about the family. There's no mother in the picture. And I don't get the whole pigeon story."

"Well, let's get on it," Chief Bloom said. "These first several hours are critical to bringing this kid back. I think we should search a ten-mile radius to start. I'll go due north." He looked at Officer Davis. "Toni, you go east, and George, you take west. We'll meet back here."

"Sounds like a plan," Officer Davis said. They headed off in their assigned directions.

Unsuccessful in their search, Jed and his friends returned to Jed's house. Jed's friends tried to comfort him

175

as he sat slumped over with his head on the patio table. His anger and frustration had turned into grief.

Nando said, "Jed, we'll find him. Or he'll come back on his own. He's a smart kid."

"I treated him too rough, Nando," Jed said. "I should have had more respect for his feelings about the birds."

"C'mon, Jed. You spend more time with him than most fathers. You taught him about racing. You share a hobby."

"He's always been a sensitive kid and I thought I should toughen him up."

"You're being too hard on yourself," Nando said. You made some good points to him. You didn't hurt any of your birds. Could you imagine if he was my son?"

"I have a bad feeling about this," Jed moaned. "The cops haven't found him and they're the experts at this."

"Well," began Nando, "the next step is a helicopter. It will only be another day or two to get one out here."

Jed groaned. "A day or two. Wherever he is, please, Lord, I hope he took enough water."

Chapter 13 – The Rescue

Woot soared high in the sky. He tried to picture Daniel's path toward Phoenix. He loaded the image in his head and flew in that same direction. As he flew, he surveyed the ground below. He was back on his game. His ability to fly gave him a big advantage over the humans. He knew he had a "bird's-eye view" and could succeed where the humans had failed. It wasn't long before he spied Daniel stuck in the boulders. Woot zoomed to the rocks in five seconds flat. "Daniel, Daniel, my buddy, I found you!"

Daniel's state had declined after another night without water. His face was screwed up with pain. He was practically delirious. But when he saw Woot, Daniel managed to speak, even in his deteriorated state. "Wha? Woot? Is that you? I can't believe it –"

Woot took in Daniel's poor condition. It made him scared. "Oh no! You're not well. We've got to get you out of here."

"I know, but how?" Daniel mumbled. "It's not like you can carry me."

Woot had an idea. "Where's your cell phone? Isn't it working?"

"No," Daniel said. "I tried to save the battery, but it died."

Woot hopped closer to Daniel, peering at him to assess his condition. He racked his brain for ideas.

But the rattlesnake had returned. While Woot was distracted looking at Daniel, the snake slithered over to the unsuspecting pigeon. Daniel didn't notice the snake either, until it was almost upon Woot. Daniel managed a sluggish warning. "Woot, be careful."

Woot whipped his head around, and in doing so, brushed it against the rattlesnake's mouth. The snake gnashed his teeth. "Stay still. You're mine or I'll bite the boy."

Woot thought fast. "Fine," Woot said. "But not in front of him. He's sick enough."

"Where then?" the snake asked.

"Follow me," Woot instructed.

Woot flew several yards away. He stayed low to the ground so that the snake could follow. He knew he could get away, but Daniel could not. Woot struggled to come up with a plan to save them both. What could he do? What would Cher Ami do? Suddenly, he heard a flutter of wings in the sky. It was either the worst possible luck or the best, because when he looked up, he saw Lucy the hawk. Woot treaded air and allowed the snake to catch up a bit.

"Wait for me at the bottom of this tree," Woot called down to the snake. "I'll trade you my life for the boy's, but I need a few minutes to brace myself."

The snake shook its small head in disbelief. "It's crazy how loyal you pigeons are to humans, but OK. You have five minutes."

Woot flew up, out of the rattlesnake's view, and approached Lucy. She looked at Woot with surprise. "Hey.

Didn't think I'd be seeing you again since you ditched me in Phoenix," Lucy said.

"Yeah, well, sorry about that. I guess I value my life over yours. But I do have a gesture of friendship for you now. How about a nice meal?"

Lucy looked surprised. "You changed your mind?"

"Not *me*, but I hear snake is a delicacy in many parts of the Southwest. I'm told it tastes like chicken."

Lucy was interested. "Wow, sounds great! If it's not a rattlesnake," she said.

Woot told a white lie. "No," he said. "Just a delicious garter snake."

She followed Woot to the tree where the rattlesnake was waiting in a coiled position. Before Lucy could change her mind and leave, the rattlesnake sprung. The two pigeon enemies faced each other. Woot had deployed his strategy. He soared away and left them to battle it out. Rattlesnake versus hawk.

Woot returned to Daniel. "That was a close call," Woot said.

Daniel was very pale. "Do you have any water?"

"Water? No, not that I can bring to you," Woot answered. He thought to himself, "Oh, what should I do?"

Daniel was fading. Suddenly, Woot had an idea. "Where's your backpack?" he asked.

Daniel pointed to the pack stuck a few feet away on the other side of the boulder. Woot flew over to it and stuck his head inside. He saw that in addition to his iPhone, Daniel had packed a small notepad and a pen. The old-fashioned system of taking notes had some advantages. Woot tore a piece of paper from the pad with his beak and brought it to Daniel. He flew back to the backpack for the pen. "Here, Dan! You write a message in English that explains where we are, and I'll bring it to your father. Can you retrace your steps? Can you write the general area of where we are?"

"I think so," Daniel said. "I was trying to…get to Phoenix…to Route I-10. We're probably only…ten miles away."

"It doesn't matter. The humans — your dad and his friends — can read what you write. Just write on that piece of paper that you're ten miles away from Route I-10. Describe the boulders and rock formations. That's the only way, since they can't understand me like you can."

Daniel wrote the location down on the paper. He rolled the slip of paper and inserted it into Woot's ankle band. Woot took off into the sky and flew at breakneck speed back to Jed's house.

As a racing pigeon, Woot was bred for speed and endurance. He and other racing pigeons had superior lung capacity compared with other types of pigeons. But racing pigeons had limits, and Woot was no exception. His chest ached and his heart pounded as he flapped his wings harder and harder. He wasn't sure how much time his best friend had left, so Woot knew he must fly at his top speed. He tried to draw strength by imagining his hero, Cher Ami. After all, she was *shot* and still managed to deliver her message. Woot pressed on.

After about an hour had passed, Woot didn't think he had any stamina left. Just as he thought he might collapse, Jed and Daniel's home finally came into view. It was dusk, and at first, the house looked like a miniature dollhouse surrounded by billowing orange and purple clouds. As Woot flew closer, the outlines of the pigeon loft became visible. Soon Woot could make out all the details of the house, including the patio. With one last surge of energy, he flew over the patio and saw Jed and his friends sitting with solemn expressions. Woot swooped down, landed on Jed's shoulder, and pecked Jed's neck with his beak. Jed's head snapped to attention and he stared at Woot in disbelief. Jed was dumbstruck, but Nando saw the bird, too.

"Well, I'll be danged," Nando said. "That racer looks a whole lot like your lost bird."

Jed stared at Woot until he was sure. "That *is* the lost bird. Daniel's favorite."

Jed looked Woot up and down and saw the paper stuck in his ankle band. Jed pulled it out and read it to himself. "C'mon, guys, let's go! I know where Daniel is."

The men jumped up, grabbed their belongings, and hopped onto Jed's truck. They sped off. They were quiet with anticipation during the ride. Finally, after what seemed like a lifetime to Jed, he parked his truck at the end of the dirt road connected to the boulders where Daniel lay fallen. Jed stood up in his truck and looked through his binoculars.

He spotted Daniel. Jed leapt from the truck and hit the ground running. "Daniel, son! I'm here!" he shouted.

The sound of his father's voice roused Daniel from his delirium. "Dad," he murmured.

Jed bolted up the boulders to reach his son. He got there in a flash, with Nando and Clint close behind.

"Here, drink," Jed said, as he dipped his canteen to Daniel's lips.

Nando and Clint tried to lift the boulder. At first it was too heavy.

"Here, get your arms under it," Clint instructed Nando. "Bend down and use your thigh muscles. Careful of your back."

They gave it another try. This time they were able to raise it just enough for a limb to slip through.

Jed put his arm around his son's waist and slipped him out from under the boulder.

Daniel cried out in pain. "Ow!"

Jed supported Daniel's weight as he led him slowly to the back of the truck.

Now Clint and Nando turned their attention to lifting Daniel onto the truck.

"OK," Nando said. "Gentle, gentle, on the count of three. One, two, three."

The men lifted Daniel and gently placed him on top of a blanket.

"Should we take him to the hospital?" Clint asked.

"No," Daniel moaned. "I'll be…OK. Please, I just… want to go home."

"Listen, Daniel," Jed began. "I, uh, owe you an apology. I said some stupid and harsh things."

But Daniel had fallen asleep. Jed kept talking anyway. "There's different ways to look at these things, and I, uh, guess I was stuck on how I was raised."

"Maybe culling's not the only way to go," Nando added. He wanted to be helpful.

"Your bird came through, Daniel," Jed said. "Maybe he wasn't the fastest, or the strongest, but he was the best homing pigeon I ever seen."

Conclusion – Lofty Gates

One month later, Daniel and Jed strolled along the grounds of their property. What a transformation! What had previously been a run-of-the-mill rural home and a typical over crowded, dilapidated pigeon coop was now an avian rescue and rehabilitation center. At the end of Jed's dirt road driveway, a wooden sign read "Woot's Lofty Gates." Jed had converted a couple of acres of his land into a home for hurt or homeless birds. Several beautiful, large, and well-constructed aviaries peppered the grounds.

The largest aviary was for the pigeons, since they were flighted birds. Most of the macaws and parrots had clipped wings, and their needs tended to be social. They needed one mate or a human friend. The pigeons needed ample space for exercise. Their aviary was twenty feet high, in the shape of a dome, and was constructed with half-inch wire mesh hardware cloth. The wire walls were lined with flat perches, branch perches, and nest boxes.

Several clean feeding dishes and a Mexican-style birdbath rested on the cement floor. The pigeons flew around inside with joy. A mated pair splashed in the bird bath. Woot and Hilde shared a nest box.

"This sure is a big improvement over our last digs," Spirit observed.

"That's the truth," Woot answered from the nest box.

"Hey, Woot," Spirit said. "I meant to congratulate you. Looks like you and the missus are expecting."

Hilde lifted a wing to expose an egg nestled in the box. "Just this one time, Spirit," she said. "We don't want it to get too overcrowded."

Woot flew out of the box and circled around, high up in the aviary. "This is nirvana. So much room to fly inside," he said.

Sally called up to Woot. "Do you think you'll miss it, Woot, dahlin'? Racing, that is."

Woot stole a shy glance at Hilde. "Nah, I got everything I need right here."

Back outside, Jed hammered a final nail into a beam. "There! That should do it. Looks pretty good, don't it?"

Daniel was all smiles. "It's great, Dad. And it's predator-proof. No hawks or bobcats are getting into this aviary."

They walked along the grounds admiring what they'd created together. They paused to look at a gazebo-shaped aviary that contained a rescued pair of hyacinth macaws, who snuggled on their perch.

"Who knew these birds lived so long?" Jed remarked. "Kind of sad that their owner passed away, but at least they can live out their lives here."

"And the tours we're doing pay for all the bills – right, Dad?" Daniel asked.

"Yup. It's technically a nonprofit, but it's all working out. A lot of people are interested in coming to see these birds."

Daniel and Jed moved along to the picnic table and chairs. They each reached for a cold drink from the cooler.

"Dad, do you think you're going to miss it?" Daniel asked.

"Miss what, son?"

"Racing and breeding pigeons, as opposed to just hanging out with them."

"Nah. I think hanging out with them and these other rescued birds will be enough of a hobby for me."

"Woot really blew everyone away by carrying that message, didn't he, Dad?" Daniel pointed out.

"I guess he was another Cher Ami in waiting, ready to help you." Jed looked at his watch. "Anyway, I have a surprise for you, just about now."

Cars and trucks pulled up the driveway to the front of the house. Friends from the pigeon club, as well as the

Freemans, got out of their vehicles, carrying food and drink to the picnic table. Jed turned on an old-fashioned boom box he had set up in a corner. Music blasted. Nando danced a salsa move. The pigeons in the aviary danced along with the music.

Elena arrived in an old Mustang, driven by her mother. Frankie was with her. Elena ran up to Daniel and gave him a big hug. Frankie looked around and extended his hand. "Man, this place looks cool."

"I've got to admit," Daniel said. "I'm a bit surprised to see you here."

"Yeah. Well, maybe we didn't get along too good, but I didn't want you to die in the desert. Besides, it's pretty cool what your bird did."

Daniel smiled from ear to ear. "Well, I'm glad you could make it."

"Glad you're OK. Hey, what's to eat? I'm starving!" They headed over to the picnic table together, as the pigeons danced in the aviary. Woot flew to the highest perch and took a bow. He'd brought his best friend home.

About The Author

Janice Lipsky is originally from New York and has been living in Scottsdale, Arizona for the past eleven years.

She has a PhD in social psychology and draws on her background to inform her creative writing. She loves nature, hiking, and taekwondo. She lives with four pigeons, three cats, and her husband.